"I have a proposal for you," Shaman said. "It's not a Hollywood contract type of proposal, but it's one that might interest you."

"I consider all proposals and offers," Tempest said.

It was worth a shot. "About that baby you wanted."

The silence went long. "I might want a child one day."

"Mmm. And if you decide you do, I wouldn't mind letting you try to have that baby with me."

"That's nice to know, soldier."

"I thought you might think so. But here's the hook—"

"There's always a hook with you."

"You have to marry me first. Then we'd practice," Shaman said. "I'm just saying that if you decide the bright lights aren't what you want, and that you want to see if you can handle the heat back here in Tempest, maybe I'll let you get in bed with me again, with that intent in mind."

"Well, that is an offer I'll have to consider," Tempest said. "Considering I've been chasing you all this time, cowboy."

Dear Reader,

The Callahan Cowboys series is such a pleasure to write! I really enjoy the journey of these cowboys and their friends—I hope you do, too!

In this story, we find that Shaman Phillips, who wants peace and quiet more than anything, has taken over his brother Gage's job. He's content to live at Dark Diablo and give himself some time to lick his war wounds— that is, until the most beautiful woman he's ever seen finds her way to the ranch. Tempest Thornbury seems to want him—but why she's attracted to a beast like him, Shaman just can't figure. Tempest brings him a lot of wonder and peace he thought he'd never feel again; giving his heart to her feels easier than he ever imagined it could be. Yet he's well aware the gorgeous blonde has no desire to tie herself to the town whose name she bears—and there are plenty of secrets she's keeping safely hidden away in her heart. Is there any way Shaman can convince Tempest that protecting her—and her heart—is the one job this warrior wants more than anything?

Writing about the Callahans and the Phillipses is like coming home for me. I hope you find a little sliver of home among these pages, and that wherever you are, you find the happiness you deserve.

Best always,

Tina Leonard

The Cowboy Soldier's Sons

TINA LEONARD

HARLEQUIN®
entertain, enrich, inspire™

Recycling programs
for this product may
not exist in your area.

ISBN-13: 978-0-373-75422-9

THE COWBOY SOLDIER'S SONS

Copyright © 2012 by Tina Leonard

www.Harlequin.com

Printed in U.S.A.

ABOUT THE AUTHOR

Tina Leonard is a *USA TODAY* bestselling author of more than forty projects, including a popular thirteen-book miniseries for Harlequin American Romance. Her books have made the Waldenbooks, Ingram and Nielsen BookScan bestseller lists. Tina feels she has been blessed with a fertile imagination and quick typing skills, excellent editors and a family who loves her career. Born on a military base, she lived in many states before eventually marrying the boy who did her crayon printing for her in the first grade. Tina believes happy endings are a wonderful part of a good life. You can visit her at www.tinaleonard.com.

Books by Tina Leonard

HARLEQUIN AMERICAN ROMANCE

No book is ever dreamed in a vacuum, and I have lots of help. Many thanks to Kathleen Scheibling, editor nonpareil, and Laura Barth, who gently keeps me in line. Also my darling and fearless agent, Roberta Brown. Much love to my cheerleading family, who always put me first, and a special thanks to the readers, who have made my career a dream come true.

Chapter One

We are such stuff as dreams are made on.
> —Shakespeare's *The Tempest*

Shaman Phillips wasn't expecting a blonde bombshell to show up at the front door of the Dark Diablo farmhouse, but one glance at her shapely legs, long silky hair and beautiful face made him believe tonight might be a lucky night for a lone wolf. "Hello," he said. "Can I help you?"

"Hi."

Shaman decided the voice of an angel went with her amazing looks. She was way out of his league—and yet even a man with scars liked to gaze at beautiful things.

"I'm looking for Chelsea Myers."

"Ah. The Chelsea Myers who married my brother Gage in July. She's Chelsea Phillips now." Shaman leaned forward, out of the doorway, planting his well-worn boots on the porch. "They live at the Callahan place, Rancho Diablo, in Diablo."

The goddess stepped closer, her high fire-engine-red heels clicking on the wood porch. "My name is Tempest Thornbury. I met Chelsea and Cat in July, before I returned to Italy." She held up a small Louis Vuitton bag, complete with tufts of tissue paper coming out the top.

Shaman knew what Louis Vuitton was; his sister, Kendall, was a huge fan. "I brought this for Cat. Is there a possibility you could give it to her?"

"Come on in," Shaman said, tamping down the wolf-like tendencies fighting inside him. "I'll get their address and you can send it to her. It'd probably be quicker. I never know when I'll see them, now that the school year has started."

Tempest smiled. "Thank you."

Shaman went to get the address, and she followed him into the house. He handed her a piece of paper. "Cat started school in the middle of August in Diablo. She's real happy there."

"I'm so glad."

He decided his visitor was even more beautiful close up. The hot-red suit fit her curves to perfection. She didn't wear a wedding ring or jewelry, just some gold hoop earrings that kissed her cheeks.

"She's a sweet girl," Tempest added.

Shaman nodded, suddenly uncomfortable and not sure why. His first thought was to seduce this angel—what man could resist?—but she was too perfect for him. How dumb was that?

Ten years in the military, most of them spent in Iraq and Afghanistan, might have left him hungry for female companionship, but it had also left him with scars on his back, a chunk missing from his shoulder and a red slash across his sun-browned cheek. He was lucky those were his only visible scars. Many of his buddies hadn't fared so well.

A little less perfection in a woman would suit him better. "Sorry I couldn't be more help."

Tempest smiled and turned on her heel. "I was hoping to see Cat and Chelsea, but I suppose they won't be back until the semester is over?"

"Can't say." He wasn't familiar with Cat's routine. "Chelsea and Gage just announced that they're expecting a baby, so I don't know how often Chelsea will be out here."

Tempest glanced back at him, looking pleased. "That's wonderful! I'm glad to hear it." She opened the front door before he could do so. "I didn't get your name?"

"Shaman Phillips." He held the door for her, and as she walked out, caught a tease of a light flowery perfume. "You staying in Tempest, Tempest?" He grinned. "I didn't realize you were named after the town."

She leaned into him, catching him off guard. "It's a stage name. My real name is Zola Cupertino."

His brain tried to process that information, along with the distracting fact that she was dangerously close to him. And he didn't think it was an accident. If he didn't know better, he'd think she—

"Soldier…" Tempest murmured.

"Yes, ma'am?" he said, out of habit. She must have seen his military bag, and his combat boots in the living room.

"I just got off a plane from Italy," she announced. "I wonder if you might be interested in taking me out to dinner?"

He blinked. "Certainly," he said, trying to be chivalrous and not sound as surprised as he was by her unexpected invitation.

She smiled at him, a sweet, slow, sexy smile, her angelic eyes free of artifice, but holding a silent plea.

Maybe he didn't want to see it. But she was still standing oh-so-close to him, and the next thing he knew, he'd taken the statuesque blonde in his arms and was kissing her like a dying man.

She kissed him back hungrily.

"Wait a second," Shaman said. He was a lucky guy, but not this lucky. Angels didn't just drop from the sky into his hard-edged world. "How did you say you know Gage and Chelsea?"

"Met them this summer. Don't stop what you're doing, soldier."

He kissed her again, his mind trying to find the hook in the sweet deal she seemed to be offering him. She could have any guy in the world. Why would she choose him, instead of running from the sight of his scar-streaked face?

What the hell. A man didn't get too many gifts in life, and if this angel wanted to fly into his arms, he needed to quit acting like a skittish horse. "Hey, you want that dinner or not?" he asked, giving her one last chance to back away.

"After," she murmured, melting into him.

He carried her to his bedroom, taking his sweet time, being careful with the soft suit and delicate white camisole. Her bra and panties were angel-wing white and breathlessly lacy, the kind that didn't do much for support but everything for a man's libido. Keeping the lights low, he whispered to her in soothing tones, expecting at any moment for her to tell him she wanted out of his bed. But she let him do whatever he wanted to her, and she was sweet like he'd never tasted sweet before.

And when he finally entered her, Shaman thought he'd

died and gone to some magical place he'd never known existed. In all the dirty, lonely nights he'd been scared out of his wits—and he'd been plenty scared, tough guy or not—he'd fantasized about a woman. Any woman. A soft, sweet woman to take away the pain.

This woman was a velvet-soft gift from the gods, and whatever he'd done to deserve this time with her, Shaman wanted the moment to last forever.

Tempest cried his name, and he lost himself in her. She grabbed at his shoulders, and he didn't even think about his wounds or his scars. He held her and kissed her, savoring her like a treasure.

Then they slept—maybe for an hour; he wasn't certain. A glance out the window showed a moon that was huge and high in the sky. Getting out of bed, he said, "Let me shower. I'll take you for that dinner."

She smiled at him in the moonlight. "Thanks, soldier."

Afraid to keep the lady waiting, he took the world's fastest shower, dressing like a madman. Yet he wasn't all that surprised when he came out and all that was left on the bed was the little Louis Vuitton bag, and a note that read, *"Just remembered I have a meeting in town. Rain check for the dinner? Tempest."*

He grunted. She'd signed the note as if it was an autograph for a book or a photo. "A meeting," he muttered. Shaman glanced at the note again, massively disappointed. *Rain check.*

I'll just bet.

"WHO IS HE?" Tempest asked her dearest friends, Shinny and Blanche Tuck, after they'd hugged each other. It was so good to be here, in the Ice Cream Shoppe where she'd spent so many happy hours. The couple had been parents of sorts, shepherding her through difficult times as a child. Shinny could always be counted on to give her one of his delicious "specials," a frothy chocolate milkshake she'd adored as a kid. Now she knew he'd simply been trying to put meat on her scrawny bones, but back then she'd thought she was the luckiest girl in the world when he gave her the scrumptious treats.

Shinny and Blanche sat across from her in the lipstick-red booth. The store was closed, and soon they'd go home. But for now they were enjoying catching up.

"He's one of the Phillips boys from Hell's Colony," Blanche said. "Seems to be a good family, if his brother Gage is any indication."

Shinny was happy to let his wife tell the story, but filling in the details was his forte. His balding head with its white tufts of hair shone under the fluorescent bulb overhead as he leaned back in the booth. "Gage comes out every once in a while. Shaman and he are trying to fix up Dark Diablo. They're the ones Jonas Callahan hired to bring the place to a working condition."

"Why'd you go there?" Blanche asked worriedly. "You don't want to be around Dark Diablo. Nothing good can come of it, even with him there."

Tempest conceded she wasn't quite sure what had happened tonight. Seduction wasn't her style, and she hadn't had a lover in years. But the man at the ranch had seemed so defenseless, so...sexy. Sexier than any guy she'd ever seen, in some way she couldn't identify. His coffee-colored eyes had had a faraway, lonely, almost vulnerable look in them, and for some reason she'd sensed in him a safe harbor. "I wanted to take Cat a present. I thought she and

Chelsea would be there. Funny that everything changed in the two months I was gone."

"Yes," Blanche said, her tall dark updo quivering under the light. She had enough hair to make up for Shinny's lack of it. "Gage and Chelsea decided living at Rancho Diablo would be best, to help Cat make the transition to the area. She adores being around all the Callahan children. We went to their wedding, by the way. It was so lovely." Her friends looked at her. "It's the kind of thing I hope you'll have one day."

"Oh." Tempest shook her head and stood. "I don't think so, Blanche. But thank you for always wanting the best for me." She looked down fondly at the people who'd been like family to her. "May I rent the bed-and-breakfast from you for a few days?"

"No," Shinny said, standing in turn. "You may stay there free of charge. It's your home, now that you're back."

Tempest gazed out the window for a moment, thinking of her villa in Italy and the job she'd been offered in New York. She hadn't planned to come out of her self-induced retirement, but something in her had said it was time to go home for a visit.

While Tempest had been living a life few people would ever experience, Shinny and Blanche had this small ice cream and soda shop, and a tiny adobe bungalow they sometimes rented as a B and B. They worked like crazy for the little they had.

They were getting older, and Tempest felt they should be slowing down. Most folks their age would be thinking about retiring. Of course, her dear friends didn't burn out from their careers, as she had.

But they were so happy to see her that just looking at their faces revived her. Made her remember that changing from the dull moth Zola Cupertino to the butterfly Tempest Thornbury was something that mattered to people who were important to her. And somehow that pride invigorated her, made her want to swim in starshine again instead of burying herself at her villa. "Either you let me pay or I'll have to find someplace else to stay."

Blanche shooed her to the door, after handing her a key. "We'll talk about money another time. Until then, you go rest. And if I were you, I'd stay away from Dark Diablo." She looked at Tempest in concern. "There's no reason to dig up bad memories by going out there."

Tempest hugged Blanche. "It's all right. Don't worry about me."

"We do." Shinny wrapped the two of them in his big, beefy arms.

Tempest closed her eyes for a moment, enjoying the closeness. "I'm fine," she said. "Truly. Thank you for letting me stay with you." She went out the door, seeing that the moon hadn't changed a bit since she'd left the cowboy soldier. *Only in Tempest does time never seem to move.*

She got into her rental car and drove around back, parking it in the garage of the only place that had ever seemed like "home" to her, a small southwestern, Pueblo-style adobe house that was clean and spare. It felt wonderful to unpack her bag, take a quick shower and melt into the soft bed.

Recalling the hungry way Shaman had kissed her warmed Tempest, settling her into a hazy place between wakefulness and slumber. Shinny and Blanche thought he was a solid man, a good man, if a loner. Tempest herself was a recluse, had been for years. Maybe that's what she'd responded to—the sense of isolation people sometimes chose when they didn't feel they deserved better.

He deserved better than her.

TWO DAYS LATER, Shaman hadn't left Dark Diablo for even a grocery run. He had too much to do. So he stayed put, even though lust prodded him to go hunt down the beautiful woman who'd seduced him with sweet kisses.

He didn't allow himself to think about her much—just about five hundred times a day. Instead, he worked on the barn Gage was determined to have torn down, and he spent time breaking the new mare Jonas Callahan had bought. Her name was Candy, but she was anything but sweet. Jonas was determined that this ebony mustang he'd gotten from a horse rescue society might be the basis for his equine program. He said she reminded him of the black Diablo mustangs that were rumored to run through the canyons of Rancho Diablo, but Shaman wasn't sure Candy had anything mystical or magical in her. She was bad-tempered and stubborn, maybe not even a diamond in the rough.

Only Jonas would want a wild mustang for his equine program. Not exactly a quality ride—and yet Shaman relished the chance to learn, and to shape the animal's spirit. It had to be done just right: slowly, patiently.

One thing a man learned in the military was patience.

He ran his hand lightly over the mare's neck, making certain the lead rope wasn't too tight. She did have a shiny coat and beautiful brown eyes. It was the attitude that he had to work on.

"Hi."

When Shaman heard the voice behind him, he knew at once that it belonged to the sweet angel who'd ditched him.

"Easy, Candy," he said, taking his time turning to face his visitor. She was dressed in blue jean capris and a filmy pink top today, a sexy dream destined to keep him sleepless. "Hello, Cupertino."

She seemed surprised by what he'd called her. He shrugged. It was her name, and he wasn't much for anything fake. "What brings you out here?"

She held up a picnic basket. It was high noon and hot; he was sweaty and had been alone with his thoughts too long. "The rain check," she said. "I'm sorry I had to leave the other night."

"No, you're not." He ignored the basket and gently tugged Candy forward by the lead rope. The mare didn't seem too disposed to be pliable, and Shaman moved carefully so she wouldn't shy away. "But that's okay. I'm not much of a guy for talking during meals."

"So I've heard."

He ignored that, too, drawing Candy in a circle. "What's in the basket?"

"Veggie wraps, made by Shinny and Blanche. Cheese and crackers. Some white wine. White-chocolate pretzels and strawberries. They said you and your family are vegetarian."

He kept the woman waiting for a few minutes, drawing out his surrender to her. Candy kicked up a hoof, trying to show him that she might be on a lead, but that didn't mean she was giving up any of her sassy spirit.

"Sounds good," he finally said. "Why don't you take it into the kitchen, put it on the table and leave it for me?"

She stared at him. "I…know you're not much for conversation, but I'd really hoped…"

He looked at her directly, daring her to be honest. "Hoped for what?"

After a moment, she said, "I'm not sure."

She wasn't being honest. And he demanded honesty. "Just leave it in the kitchen," he told her. "Tell Shinny and Blanche thanks. And I sent your bag to Cat this morning, with Jonas."

"Thank you," she said. "I didn't mean to leave it here."

"Yeah, you did." He wasn't going to give her an inch.

She didn't say anything, and he felt her indecision. After a minute, the tall, gorgeous blonde carried the picnic basket to the farmhouse, disappearing inside. He stayed outside with Candy, never looking toward the house, yet listening for the sound of her white Land Rover to start up. After thirty minutes, when he didn't hear it, he put Candy away with a hose-down she despised and a rub she tried to kick him for as her equine thank-you. Then he let her go, after putting out hay for her to eyeball with wild eyes. She galloped off to forage for herself—but he knew she'd remember that treats were here and always available after training.

She'd remember, and she'd have to make up her mind to cool her attitude just a bit, day by day.

He went inside the house, took off his boots. The picnic basket wasn't on the table. Instead, the table had been set, with white wine in the glasses. Tempest was asleep on the sofa, her long, silky hair falling over her shoulder.

He could stand here all day, doing nothing more than stare at her.

But she hadn't come here to be stared at.

"Cupertino," he said, "wake up."

She came awake, her big blue eyes widening when she saw him standing over her. "Thanks for the grub," he said. "Either you go now or you stay. If you stay, know that I intend to love you like you've never been loved."

She didn't move, but kept her wide eyes locked on his, with that same angelic look she'd worn two nights before.

"Fair warning," he said, taking her hand and drawing her from the sofa. "Get the strawberries. I'm in the mood for something sweet."

She made a move to do as he requested, but when he started slowly undoing the buttons on her blouse, she didn't pull away. Shaman kissed her, ravaging her mouth, not bothering to hide the fact that he wanted her like mad. She moaned, and he murmured, "Rain check later," and carried her down the hall.

TWO WEEKS LATER, Shaman waved to the demolition crew who'd come to raze the barn, his brother Gage standing nearby to help oversee it with him. Today was the day, a big day. Finally, they could begin the complete rebuilding of Dark Diablo. Tearing down the barn and bunkhouse was necessary in the vision Jonas Callahan had for his vast acreage.

It was good to tear down old and build new. Cleared out ghosts.

"What is that?" Gage demanded, his vision not on the crew's heavy equipment, as it should have been, but on the fabulous blonde leaving the farmhouse after a very satisfying night spent in Shaman's arms.

"Looks like a woman to me," he said. "Focus, bro. We've got a job to do here."

"I know it's a woman. In fact, I know *who* it is." Gage stared at him. "What I want to know is why she's here."

Shaman shrugged. "Cupertino hangs around on occasion, brings me a meal or two."

His brother was agog. "Not you."

He shrugged again. "Guess so."

They watched the blonde get in her Land Rover and drive away. Shaman always hated to see her go. He never knew if she'd return. She usually came around dinnertime, and stayed through the night, letting him worship her between the sheets.

Sometimes she didn't return for a day or two, and that always worried him. One day she'd get tired of him, a simple man with not much to offer, and he would never see her again. Whatever demons she was exorcising out of her soul were nothing she cared to talk about. In fact, the two of them didn't do much talking.

"Listen," his brother said. "Tempest is not someone you just toy with. That is a very kind woman. Cat and Chelsea consider her a friend."

"Yeah." Shaman liked her, too. His gaze went back to the giant bulldozer about to push into the enormous old barn. "She's real nice."

"No, no." Gage shook his head. "You don't understand. Tempest is a good woman."

"I got that. You're getting twisted up for nothing, bro. Listen, Cupertino brings me dinner. I guess she thinks I'm starving. And I say thanks, because the truth is, she's a darn good cook. And I like to look at her." He shook his head. "You can't expect me to turn that down."

Gage was clearly astonished. After a minute, he said, "You call her Cupertino?"

"That's her name."

"But do you know who she is?" he demanded.

"She's a woman who grew up in Tempest." Shaman didn't see what the big deal was. It wasn't like he was sending out engraved invitations begging her to come by. She showed up when she wanted, she left when she wanted.

"She's in negotiation right now for a starring role in a major Broadway production that might be turned into a movie, for one thing," his brother told him.

"Is she?" Shaman watched the bulldozer tear into the first wall, collapsing it. Dust and bits of wood flew everywhere.

"If you'd read the newspaper, you'd know that," Gage said. "The *New York Times* publishes a Sunday edition that's really quite informative, if you cared to learn about the world around you."

He laughed. "The paperboy must have left me off the route."

"Online *Times* is just fine. You can read it every day. Takes very little effort. You get twenty free articles the first month, and if you decide you like being informed about the world outside of your shell, you can subscribe. It's great."

"Yeah, well. There's no internet here. If you haven't noticed, we're miles from civilization." And Shaman didn't really care. He liked the setup just the way it was. He didn't want to know more about the woman than he did. Whatever it was that she wanted from him, it suited him well.

"There is internet," Gage stated. "In fact, the internet is how Cat found Tempest in the first place."

That caught Shaman's attention. "Our niece wrote her?"

"Yes. Cat wanted Tempest to come home. She thought my wife's writing creativity would get a boost if she met Tempest. Cat had other reasons for choosing her for pen pal status, but that's the main idea. So don't tell me the internet doesn't work. It's what brought her all the way from Italy."

"Doesn't matter. She'll go to her gig when she's ready. In the meantime, she doesn't look like she's suffering, does she?" Shaman asked, crossing his arms. "I mean, if you're trying to infer that she can do better than me, I'll be the first to admit I'm no prince, bro."

Gage shook his head. There probably would have been more discussion of the wonders of the woman who seemed to want nothing more than nights in Shaman's arms, but two walls collapsed on the barn, and workers started yelling and running around, ending the debate.

Thankfully. Because if he heard any more about what a goddess she was, he was going to have to tell her to take her picnic basket and hit the road. Shaman knew that, like the beast in the fairy tale, you should just appreciate the pretty things in life—while in the back of your mind you heard your mother saying, "Don't touch anything in the store! You might break it." You heard your father say, "A woman only wants a man with money and power."

One day it'll be over.

Right now, I just try to make her happy.

Chapter Two

"We're going to have to quit meeting like this." Shaman got out of bed, glancing back at the beautiful blonde gracing his sheets.

Tempest rose, too, dragging the sheet with her. If he had more time, he'd consider snatching it off her and tumbling them both back into bed.

"Shaman," she said, "it's not forever."

He wondered what was happening about her negotiations for the Broadway show, but wasn't about to ask. She'd never mentioned her career, so presumably it was something she didn't care to discuss, at least not with him. "Yeah," he said. "Forever's a tough thing to plan."

She smiled. "I'm going to get dressed."

He turned away. "Be my guest. The workers arrived about ten minutes ago, so I'm going to head out."

"Thanks." She took her sheet into the bathroom with her, wrapped toga-style, goddesslike. He stared at the door for a long moment, briefly pondering taking her in the shower, then decided maybe she wouldn't welcome that. These "visitations" of hers were strictly on her terms.

He finished dressing and took off for the barn, snag-

ging a bagel from the stash Tempest had put on the
counter.

Then again, one never knew which visit would be
the last. He was not a man to look at destiny without a
measure of appreciation—and she *had* mentioned "not
forever," though they'd never talked about the future before. A warning sensation shifted inside him, a prickling
of unease. Intuition was a powerful thing, whether in
looking out for mines and roadside bombs, or knowing
that eventually a woman like her was ready to move on.

"What the hell," Shaman said, and went back inside
to appreciate the best thing that had happened to him
in years.

IT HAD BEEN TWO DAYS since she'd seen Shaman. Tempest
was trying to figure out why spending time with him was
beginning to matter so much to her. He was kind and
strong, qualities that really called to her.

But she needed distance. Deeply felt the need for some
space. So today she was renewing a special friendship instead of concentrating on hunky cowboys. She'd brought
Cat Phillips, Shaman's niece, to share a Shinny "special"
with her. The change in the teen from sullen to happy
heartened Tempest, made her yearn for the same sort of
carefree joy in her own life.

"My dad says," Cat Phillips began, settling into the
red-lipstick-colored booth, "that you're a short-timer."

She smiled at the teen. "A short-timer here in Tempest?"

Cat nodded, slurping the chocolate milkshake Shinny
had made. "Dad says this is too much of a backwater
for you. He says that even if you do like Uncle Shaman,

you won't stay because there's nothing here." The teen shrugged. "I thought that once, too. Now I think there's lots here."

"It's good that your father talks to you so much," Tempest said, not really wanting to speak about the short-timer tag that had been hung on her.

"He didn't talk to me about you and Uncle Shaman," Cat said. "I heard him telling Chelsea that he doesn't expect you to be around much longer, which is a good thing, because he doesn't want Shaman to break your heart."

Tempest blinked. "Really."

"Mmm." The girl nodded, her freshly bobbed black hair moving as she eagerly reached for the cookies Shinny's wife, Blanche, placed in front of them before heading away from their booth. "Dad says Uncle Shaman is damaged goods, for one thing, now that he's been in the military so long. He also says my uncle's stubborn as hell, and he won't do anything but hide out at Dark Diablo."

"I'm a little reclusive at times myself," Tempest said. "It's not always a bad thing."

"Yeah, but Dad says Aunt Kendall and Uncle Xav are bugging him to get Shaman home. They say he refuses to even discuss it while you're in town."

Tempest hesitated. "Where is Shaman's home?"

"In Texas. Hell's Colony." Cat squinted, obviously thinking. "It's kind of a palace."

"A palace?" Tempest couldn't envision Shaman in a palace. He seemed as one with the outdoors, fully connected to ranch life.

"Kind of." She shrugged, fumbling for a description. "But anyway, Dad says the pressure's on for Shaman to go home, though when he brings it up, Uncle Shaman tells him to get bent. I'm not supposed to say *get bent*." Cat shrugged. "But it's what Dad said."

Tempest hated to be part of any discord in Shaman's life. He was kind to her, and she enjoyed their time together. She didn't want Cat upset, either. She was fond of the girl, and if it hadn't been for her, Tempest knew she might not ever have returned to the small town where she'd grown up—and had such an unhappy childhood.

Yet it was best to face things one had ignored too long. "I feel badly that your father thinks I'm keeping your uncle from his family."

"No," Cat said. "Chelsea said Uncle Shaman wouldn't go home anyway, and that Dad had been plenty hard to rope back into the fold himself, so he needed to butt out of Shaman's life. And then I think Dad must have agreed, because I heard a lot of snacking going on after that." She looked at Tempest wisely. "Snacking is what I call it when Daddy's smooching on Chelsea. Lots of little snacking noises."

Tempest smiled. "I'm glad they're happy."

"They are. We all are. I love Rancho Diablo!" Cat grinned, her pert little face shining with delight. "I like Dark Diablo, too, but there's no kids. Dad says Uncle Shaman needs some ankle-biters to tie him to one place, and Chelsea said he'd better tend to his own ankles before he worried about his brothers' and sister's."

"I heard you're going to be a big sister," Tempest said.

"I am. I can't wait! Of course, I won't be able to come visit as often, once I have my brother or sister." She again looked at Tempest with those wise eyes. "I'll miss you, but I'll be very busy taking care of the baby, you know."

Tempest grinned, delighted with the changes in the

once-angsty Cat. "I know. I understand completely. If I had a baby, I would want you to be my chief babysitter."

"Maybe you'll have a baby one day, Tempest," Cat said. "There's Dad, so I have to go. He said he'd drop me off for a visit only if I came right out when he was ready to leave. He said it wouldn't take long for him to pound the stuffing out of Uncle Shaman, and then we had to hit the road. He doesn't like to be away from Chelsea for long. Thank you again for the cool headband you gave me. I really love it." She hugged her, a good, strong hug that warmed Tempest, then ran to say goodbye to Shinny and Blanche. "Goodbye! Thank you for the delicious ice cream!"

They waved at the thin teen as she ran out the door. From the window, Tempest watched as Cat jumped into her father's truck.

"She never fails to brighten our day," Shinny said, coming over to take Cat's seat. "That is one happy little girl."

Tempest nodded. "Yes, she is."

"Funny, but I think you had a part in that," he added.

Tempest looked at the older gentleman regarding her with smiling eyes. "Cat made all her changes on her own."

"Yeah, but you believed in her enough to come back to town. It means a lot to kids when people they admire notice them."

Tempest remembered when Cat had been a sadder version of herself. "She has good parents now."

Shinny nodded. "She reminds me of you, in a way."

"I don't know." Tempest swirled the straw in her milkshake, not really feeling like thinking about her own childhood. "Is there anything I can do to help you, before I go?"

"Nope." Shinny patted her hand. "You go rest. Blanche and I'll see you at dinner."

Nodding, she got up and gave him a kiss on his almost-bald head, then left the shop. She wondered why Gage would want to pound the stuffing out of his brother, then decided it didn't have anything to do with her.

IT WAS NOT SHAMAN'S BEST day.

First, Gage had run by with a full head of steam to rag all over him about the barn contractor—who Gage had fired. Jonas Callahan didn't like the contractor's vision—and now it was up to Shaman to figure out what was in Jonas's head. In spite of that, this job was a great one to oversee, so he had no quibbles. He just wanted it to go more smoothly than it was, given that his boss had just changed his mind about everything.

Bosses tended to do that, and he'd suffered enough annoyed superior officers to take an occasional ear-bending in stride.

Still, he could have used a break in the action before the land mine that was his sister drove onto the ranch. From the roof of the farmhouse, Shaman could see Kendall's car edging up the drive. He knew it was her because she was driving a black Land Rover. It seemed the whole family fleet had been replaced with matching black Land Rovers, if Gage had the information right. Gil Phillips, Inc., was all about uniformity.

He sat on the roof, watching Kendall as she got out of her car. She wore a ladylike cream-colored skirt and jacket, and turquoise-blue sky-high heels. Some things never changed.

"Hi," she called up to him.

"Howdy."

"Get the hell off the roof, please. It's dangerous."

He laughed. "This isn't dangerous. I know dangerous, and I'll tell you when I see it."

She was annoyed, he could tell. "We need to talk."

Obviously, since she'd driven over from Hell's Colony. "You have a cell phone. Doesn't it work?" He climbed down the ladder, deciding it was best to obey his little sister when she was in her bossy element.

"Mom wants you to come home," Kendall said, following him inside.

Shaman washed his hands at the sink, his mind on the condition of the farmhouse roof. It had occurred to him that if Jonas was going to hire a contractor who would subcontract out the roofs for the outbuildings, maybe getting this one replaced at the same time would be financially expedient. In his opinion, it was badly needed.

"I'm sorry. What did you say?" He looked at his sister.

Kendall sat on the old leather-topped stool in front of the counter. "Mom wants you to come home."

"Because?"

"Because you can do this kind of work there. She says you spent enough years away in the military." His sister's face softened as she looked at him. "We miss you."

"I miss you, too, but this is my job."

"You have a job. It's called Gil Phillips, Inc.," she reminded him.

"This is a paying job, something not all of my friends

have been able to find once they got back to the States. Besides, haven't you heard you can never go home?"

Kendall gave him a look of disgust. "That's for other people. Our home represents our livelihood."

Shaman smiled at her. "Not mine."

"You're being difficult, Shaman. What is it about this place that has you and Gage so obsessed?" She glanced around the airy kitchen. "Really, it's kind of a dump."

"It's actually pretty nice." He thought the farmhouse was quiet and cheerful. Mostly it was quiet, and that he needed.

"I do not understand." Kendall shrugged delicately. "This place could use a decorator."

"I'll put your name into the hat for Jonas Callahan."

"Don't you dare." She slid off the stool, walking around the kitchen. "You need to come home. Xav's decided to get married."

Shaman blinked. "To whom?"

"To some gold digger. Mom is up in arms."

"What does that have to do with me?" He tossed the dish towel he'd used onto the counter. "Xav's life is his own."

"Mom wants you to talk sense into him."

Shaman shook his head. "Not me. I leave all the gold digger talks in your capable hands." If Xav's sweetie wasn't appropriate in some way, he figured Kendall would have her wrapped up in so much legal tape she'd barely be able to move.

"Mom thinks it would be better coming from you. Older, wiser brother."

"No, what might have helped is if Xav had ever been able to get out from under your and Mom's hands. And purse strings. Seeing the world doesn't hurt a man." Although sometimes it *had* hurt him, Shaman amended silently. Sometimes it had hurt a lot. But he was tougher for it, too.

Kendall gave him a look that was distinctly displeased. "Shaman, Xav looks up to you—"

A knocking at the door stopped her words, for which Shaman was glad. The last thing he was going to do was get involved in a family issue. He opened the door, his whole day brightening at the sight of Tempest on his porch. "Hi, Cupertino."

"Hi."

He didn't open the door wider, but noted that she had her picnic basket, so dinner was about to be served. And maybe dessert as well. This was good. Lately, he had a sense of unease that everything in their relationship was about to change. She'd seemed a bit distant somehow, and he'd been bracing himself.

It felt great just to look at her, and know she'd come back one more time.

"Your niece came by to see me," Tempest said.

"Oh?" Shaman didn't open the door any farther, trying to keep Tempest and his sister apart as long as possible, reluctant for his two worlds to collide.

"Yeah. She thinks I should have a baby," Tempest said, clearly teasing. From behind him, Shaman heard, "Oh, great, just great," from Kendall.

"Do you have company?" Tempest tried to look around him. "I saw the car, but I thought it was—"

"It's mine." Kendall glanced around Shaman's shoulder, then gave him a little shove to get him out of her way. She was nothing if not determined. "Is there a baby in that basket? Or are you just looking for a husband?"

"Kendall," Shaman said, "back off, sister, dear. Come in, Tempest. Join the dysfunctional family."

Kendall sniffed, checking her out as Tempest entered. Both women were blonde and gorgeous, but there was no doubt that Tempest was taller and more statuesque. Still, neither of them would look bad on a magazine cover.

"Girls, girls, there's no need to fight. Kendall wants me to go home, and you want to have a baby. Can't we work things out?"

Tempest put her basket on the counter and began pulling things from it. "Doesn't sound like it. However, I just happened to bring enough for three." She looked at Kendall, who was still bristling. "You can join us. That is, if you eat."

"I eat." She came over to check out Tempest's menu. "Is that Brie?"

"It is. And this is a light, crisp white wine, if you drink that. Also, this is sliced avocado on wheat, if you eat avocado. Some caviar, if you know what that is."

"I do," Kendall snapped. She took a plate from Tempest and helped herself to the repast. "I guess if you're stalking a man for a baby, at least you bring decent bait."

Shaman laughed. "Kendall, you haven't changed a bit."

"Oh?" Tempest looked up from making a plate for him. "She doesn't get out of her cage often?"

He couldn't help laughing harder. The outraged look on Kendall's face was too perfect. "Be sweet to my overprotective sister, Tempest. She means well." He kissed Kendall's cheek, then Tempest's. "Now you girls make up, because I say so. And I appear to be the rooster in the henhouse today."

"Whatever," Kendall said. "She just has unusual opening lines."

"You have a big mouth," Tempest said pleasantly. "I could probably recommend a voice coach for you."

Shaman happily ate the grub Tempest had brought him. "So, we're going to have to work some things out. One, I'm not going home, Kendall, no matter what's happening at the old haunt. And two, I'm not interested in having a baby, Cupertino." He gazed at both of them, deciding he was a lucky guy to have two ladies that cared about him, sort of. "So what else did our niece have on her mind?"

Tempest shook her head. "Cat is happy as can be."

"Come on," Kendall said, munching on the avocado-laden toast. "Don't hold back just because of me."

"She said Gage had come over to pound the stuffing out of you," Tempest admitted to Shaman. "I thought I better check on you and make sure you weren't incapacitated."

Both siblings laughed.

"Gage wishes he could pound the stuffing out of you?" Kendall looked at her brother. "What's got him out of sorts, anyway?"

"I don't know. This job, I guess." Shaman didn't care right now. "Are you staying, Kendall?"

She glanced at Tempest. "No."

"Don't go because of me," Tempest said.

Kendall gave her a sour look. "I'm off to Rancho Diablo to check on my other brother, the one who isn't in hiding out here in the middle of nowhere, and my darling niece."

Shaman grinned. "You know, Kendall, if you ever got out of those power suits and let your hair down—"

"I'd find myself propositioning men for babies? I don't think so." His sister slid off the stool. "I'm only staying at Rancho Diablo for the night. I have to get back to Hell's Colony. Mom's not feeling well, and—"

"You didn't say anything about that," Shaman said.

"I shouldn't have to," Kendall retorted. "She's old. She wants her son at home. No big shock, right?"

He recognized guilt as one of Kendall's weapons, and pulled her to him so that he could rub her hair and muss it up, the way he had when they were children. And later, when they were teens. She shrieked predictably, making him grin. "That felt great," Shaman said.

Kendall grabbed her purse. "I'm glad it was good for you. If Gage does come to pound your stuffings, I hope he succeeds. Goodbye, Tempest. Was that your name?" Kendall frowned. "It fits."

Tempest smiled at her and reached out to shake hands. "Tempest Thornbury. It's nice to meet you, Kendall."

"Tempest…Thornbury?" She frowned again. "Not the Tempest Thornbury from New York, who used to sing and act on—"

"One and the same," Shaman said cheerfully, loving the shocked expression on his sister's face.

Kendall glanced at the picnic basket, then back at her. "No wonder you don't want to come home, Shaman."

He laughed. "And you thought I just spent all my time on the roof."

"I think you're crazy. But at least if she wants to have a baby, she won't be after your money, too. I guess." Kendall shook her head. "Be nice to my big brother, or I'll send mean critics after you. Love you, Shaman. Please come home soon and give Xav a man-to-man chat. This well-planted daisy is on the level of Gage's first wife, if you know what I mean. Bad all the way around."

Kendall left, a smooth slide of silk and high heels moving out the door. Shaman followed, walking her to the car, then making sure she was safely belted inside. "I love you," he told her. "I'll come home at some point. I just don't know when. And no family chats with Xav. It's his life."

"Make it soon." She drove away, and Shaman went back inside.

Tempest was pouring two glasses of wine.

"I'm glad you're here," he told her, ignoring the wine and pulling her close.

"Really?" She snuggled against his chest, and Shaman closed his eyes, loving the feel of her in his arms.

"Yes. I miss you." He kissed her hair, breathing the scent of her in. "You know, they say the way to a man's heart is through his stomach."

Tempest ground his foot under hers, which didn't do any damage because of the steel-toed work boots he wore, but he got the message. "So back to this baby talk you and Cat had."

"It was Cat's idea," Tempest said, and he said, "Oh, come now, Cupertino, teenagers don't think that kind of stuff up. Don't blame my precocious niece." He scooped her into his arms. "You carry the wine, and we'll go talk some more about how babies are made. I want to see where you're going with this."

"Soldier, I think you know just fine." Tempest grabbed the glasses and let him carry her down the hall.

Chapter Three

The funny thing was that once Tempest had mentioned "baby" to him, Shaman found himself actually thinking about it. A lot. Wasn't a man supposed to run at the thought of a woman who wanted to get pregnant with his child?

He didn't.

It had been a week since she'd been by with her picnic basket, and he was still mulling over her offhand comment. Maybe she'd been playing around. Maybe the baby suggestion had been her opening line, like sex talk. Sure, that was probably it.

It had worked. He'd made love to her all night.

A spray of water caught him in the face as he wandered around the barn, making him blink with surprise. "Cat! You little devil!"

He ran after his niece, dedicated to the idea of tossing her in the creek for her just deserts. She eluded him, jumping into the creek herself, fully dressed, and just as he began tugging off his boots to land the cannonball of all cannonballs on his niece, he realized they weren't alone.

Fiona Callahan stood a hundred yards off, grinning at Cat's square hit on her uncle. He'd bet Fiona had bought the water blaster for Cat. Seemed like something a woman who'd raised six Callahan boys would think was a necessary ingredient to childhood.

"Hi, Fiona," Shaman said. "Good to see you again."

"Don't let me stop you," she called. "I distinctly thought you were about to cannonball your niece."

The thought was so tempting. "Best to do that when she doesn't suspect," he said, wiping his face, smiling at Cat splashing gleefully in the creek. "I'm sorry she's not a happy kid."

Fiona smiled. "Yeah. Miserable."

"So, are you out here doing Jonas's bidding?"

"Pretty much." Fiona seated herself in one of the wrought-iron chairs permanently ensconced in the mushy dirt surrounding the creek. "Actually, Cat pleaded with her dad to let her come out here and see her uncle, and Tempest. I said I'd run her over here. Gage wanted to take Chelsea to the ob-gyn." Fiona pulled out a wad of knitting from the bright pink plastic bag she carried. "Don't let us keep you."

Cat had grabbed a raft and was floating on her back, gazing up at the sky, a kid with no worry that winter was on its way.

"So what does Jonas want you to tell me?" Shaman asked.

Fiona didn't look up from her knitting, studying it with a furrowed brow. One thing Shaman knew was how to knit, and he could tell she'd dropped a whole ton of stitches from her looped needles. Beginner's mistake.

"He wants the barn up before the snows come. Probably late October. He wants to bring out more horses by then." Fiona gave Shaman a kindly smile. "I thought

I'd let you know, since you're probably not aware of the weather in New Mexico."

"Jonas hasn't even chosen an architect or a plan."

"You and Gage are responsible for that." She shook her head at her knitting, perplexed.

"Jonas didn't like the first set of plans. He wanted a different architect."

"You'll get it figured out." Fiona sighed at the hot-pink ball of wool. It was a good quality yarn, but if she didn't quit ratting at it, it wasn't going to be fit for anything except lining bird nests.

"Here," Shaman said, "let me see if I can help this along for you." He sat in the wrought-iron chair next to hers and began unraveling stitches until he got to the place where she'd dropped a few. Then he reknit it. "Is this your first project?"

"It is, and I don't think I'm much of a knitter." Fiona looked depressed about that. "I was going to make my friends scarves this year, but it's not quite as easy as I hoped it would be. Where'd you learn to do that?"

"From my mother. And believe it or not, there are times when knitting soothes the savage beast." Knowing she was carefully studying his method, Shaman knitted a few more rows for good measure, then handed it back to her. "Okay, Fiona, you know as well as I do that a state-of-the-art barn can't be ready in a couple of months. Jonas needs to select the architect and the plan. I only oversee the project. Why is he handing this off to me?"

"Because your brother Gage owns a small part of the property now. It was in their agreement. Gage would work here, and in lieu of a paycheck, he'd get some acreage. So Jonas knows Gage has skin in the game. And,"

Fiona continued, "Jonas is busy. He's a father, you know, and we've stuck the mayor's hat on him, too, in Diablo." She proceeded with the knitting, moving the needles more confidently now that she'd had some tutoring. "Once it starts snowing around here, it can snow for days. Jonas wants everything ready."

"All right. I'll talk it over with Gage." Shaman would do whatever he needed to do to keep the boss man happy. "Have you already been by to see Tempest?"

Fiona nodded. "Cat says you're thinking about marrying her."

Shaman blinked. "Uh, that's news to me." He wondered if Cat had said the same to Tempest. If she had, he figured he'd never see Tempest again.

"Well, where there's smoke, there's fire. That's what we say around here," Fiona said cheerfully. "Thanks for saving the scarf. If I get good at this, I'll make you one for Christmas. Come on, Cat, honey. We've got to drive back to Rancho Diablo. I still have to whip up dinner."

His niece slogged out of the creek joyfully. "This is the most beautiful place on earth," she said, "besides Rancho Diablo. I guess you float in the creek all the time, Uncle Shaman."

He hadn't, not once. "Maybe I should."

She nodded at him solemnly. "You should."

"I'll keep that in mind. I'm glad you came by to see me, honey." He kissed her on the head. "Don't forget your water cannon. I'm going to go grab you a towel."

"It's okay. I brought extra clothes. Nana Fiona knew I wanted to take a swim."

"Bring a swimsuit next time, okay?" he said, walking them back to Fiona's truck.

"Not as much fun that way. 'Bye, Uncle Shaman!"

He waved as the ladies drove off. The sun was hanging low in the sky, a fireball harbinger of fall, and Shaman felt a tickle of unease. It was the dinner hour, long past the time when Tempest usually showed up, and the drive was empty of gorgeous blonde. And she'd been chatting with Cat, his darling niece, who dropped hints about babies and marriage like they were gumdrops in a fairy tale.

Maybe it was time he broke his self-appointed exile and did picnic basket duty.

Shinny smiled at Shaman when he made his first stop at the ice cream shop. "Howdy, cowboy!" the older man said. "We don't see you in town much. Almost never. What brings you out from Dark Diablo?"

"I'm looking for Tempest. Have you seen her?" He had no idea where she lived. In fact, he knew nothing—or very little—about her, beyond the fact that she was crazy-sexy and cooked like a dream. He didn't even have her cell phone number.

Shinny flung a hand over his shoulder, pointing to the back of the shop, Shaman guessed. "She's probably in the B and B."

"B and B?" He didn't want to admit how little he knew about Tempest, but Shinny appeared to be happy to fill in the blanks.

"What we sometimes call the guesthouse. It's really her home, when she's in town, which isn't often. You can go around back and see if she's in. She'd said she was going to be practicing, but I don't think she'd mind a break."

"Thanks, Shinny," Shaman told the shop owner. He went out the front door and headed around back, seeing Tempest's car in front of the small adobe house. He knocked on the rustic wooden door, waiting, feeling like a guy on his first date.

It would be a first date, he realized—if he could get her to go out with him.

She opened the door, clearly surprised to see him. His heart hammered as it hadn't in months, not since he'd known he was coming back to the States, and had landed at the military base almost a civilian.

"Shaman!"

He nodded. "In the flesh."

"What are you doing here?" She didn't smile, but he didn't think she was totally annoyed that he'd surprised her, either. Clearly, she had been practicing whatever it was she practiced, because she was slightly glowing. Black leggings and a white top clung to her body so tightly he nearly had a rise just looking at her.

Heck. He did. Shaman shifted, forcing his mind back to his mission. "I figured it was my turn to bring the picnic basket." He felt sort of silly saying it, but she looked at him with curiosity in her big eyes.

"So where is it?"

Where was it, indeed. "Actually, it's a picnic basket in theory. I was hoping you'd let me drag you out to Cactus Max's for a date. I hear that's the place in town to get great food."

She blinked. "You've never been there?"

He shook his head. "Pretty much I survive on what you bring out to the ranch, gorgeous."

She studied him for a long moment, which gave him

a chance to drink her in. Her blond hair was pulled up in a shining ponytail high on her head, and she wore long, dangling silver earring strands. She looked like heaven, and Shaman began to realize that this woman was much more to him than just an occasional bedmate.

"Do you want to come in?" she asked. "I've probably got something in here I could whip up for you to eat."

He certainly did. But he knew where that would lead—right into bed. And suddenly Shaman realized that Cupertino—Tempest—had no intention of ever moving their relationship beyond the bedroom. If he succumbed to the red-hot desire fogging him right now, their relationship would never be anything but casual.

And suddenly, that wasn't good enough for him anymore.

"Look, Cupertino," Shaman said, "let's eat out. It's date night."

She pursed her lips. "We could have date night here."

"No. We want to do this right." He wasn't going to skulk around with her anymore. If she didn't dig him the way he dug her, he could deal with that. But it was time to take whatever it was they were doing to the next level.

"What is it that we want to do right?"

He leaned over, kissing her on the lips. "I'm trying to date you, Cupertino, if you'd quit trying to be on top all the time."

Then he kissed her again, deeply, fully. She tasted like peppermint, and his brain was screaming at him to go through the door into the golden known, finding the pleasure with her that he craved so much. But he was pretty sure she was avoiding him, and he wanted more from her than she wanted to give.

"You make it hard to say no," Tempest said breathlessly.

"I'm trying to." Shaman leaned against the doorjamb, crossing his arms. "I'll wait while you get dressed up real pretty for me."

She arched a brow. "You don't think I'm pretty now?"

"I think you're gorgeous." He grinned at her bruised femininity. "I'll wait outside while you do whatever it is girls do before their first date."

Tempest studied him, seeming to come to a decision. "It may take me a while. You could wait the better part of an hour."

"Spoken like a true diva. I've kind of heard that about you showbiz types."

She made a face. "Hope you like waiting."

He grinned as she closed the door. It was a beautiful night, and he had nothing to do but feel smug about the fact that he was taking out the hottest woman in town. Even if she showered, powdered and sprayed for an hour, he was willing to wait for their first date night together.

She opened the door not five minutes later, dressed in blue jeans with a huge shredded hole in one knee, beat-up brown flats and a T-shirt that had New Mexico Lobos plastered across it. She wore a white cap with a blue Ralph Lauren polo horse on it, her ponytail pulled through the hole in the back. "I'm ready."

"Absolutely stunning." He kissed her on the nose. "I can't wait to take you to dinner, angel cake."

She took the arm he offered. "Not Cactus Max's, though."

"Somewhere fancier?" He helped her into his truck.

"Someplace different," Tempest said.

"Whatever you want, beautiful. The picnic basket is on your terms tonight."

Maybe there was an outdoor burger joint in town she favored. In Tempest, he figured just about any place was probably delicious—as long as he was with her.

TEN MINUTES LATER, Shaman had followed Tempest's directions to a falling-in, run-down shack off the main road. "Here?"

"This is it."

"I don't think we're going to find anything to eat here." He got out of his truck, walking up the overgrown path to the ramshackle house, careful to keep an eye on Cupertino. There was no telling what might be hiding in the dense foliage and cactus surrounding the property. It was a mess.

"There never was much to eat here," Tempest said, pushing open the front door.

Shaman wasn't surprised to see that it was practically falling off its hinges. "This is a firetrap. Wonder why it hasn't been condemned?"

Tempest didn't answer, and he moved a few fallen clumps of plaster out of her way as she moved through the dark foyer. It was as if she was mesmerized. Shaman's heart beat hard, and for some reason he wished he had one of his guns on him. He could feel the hair on the back of his neck prickling, as it always did before danger hit in the war zone.

"Hey, gorgeous," he said, reaching out to grab Tempest's hand. "Trust me, I can afford to take you to a decent hamburger joint."

She walked into the kitchen, compelling him to go

with her. He was sure he saw something skitter under one of the counters, and wondered why she wasn't frightened out of her wits.

"Someone's been here," she murmured. "Someone's living here."

Now he was truly creeped out. "I'm all for excitement, but trespassing's usually frowned on."

She turned to look at him. "This is my house."

He hesitated, glancing around him, trying to square the beautiful woman with the rattrap she claimed was hers. "I don't get it."

"This is where I grew up." Tempest shrugged. "So now you know."

He pulled her to him. "It was probably a great home in its day."

"It wasn't." She leaned against his chest. "They don't condemn this house because it's mine."

"I don't think you'll be living here," Shaman said. "Although you might consider renting it to the Munsters or the Addams Family. A Morticia type would probably really dig it."

"You don't like it? This isn't your dream home?" Tempest looked up at him. He could see her bright eyes in the darkness, and he wondered why she had brought him here.

"I like you," he said, "and I think you're hot wearing spiderwebs." He brushed one off her cap and kissed her on the nose. "You know, I bet you could convince me to—"

"What are you doing in my house?"

A man's voice erupted behind them, and Tempest shrieked, clinging to Shaman for just an instant.

Then she moved away, though he tried to shield her. "This is *my* house. What are you doing here?"

A flashlight shone on her, cutting the darkness. "Zola?"

She stepped closer, though Shaman tried to hold her back. "Bobby Taylor?"

"Yeah." He shone the beam at Shaman. "Who's he?"

"Never mind." Tempest snatched the flashlight from the man, nearly giving Shaman a heart attack. She shone it in the guy's face. "What are you doing in my house?"

"I'm staying here. And it's not like you need this joint, sister."

Chapter Four

Tempest put the flashlight on the counter so the beam pointed to the ceiling, illuminating the room with a small circle of light. "I'm not your sister, Bobby."

She felt Shaman move closer to her, and was warmed by the protection she knew he offered. But she could handle this.

"Don't want him to know?" Bobby jerked his head toward Shaman. "Zola's mom had a *special* relationship with my father, Bud. She's the love child. So yes, Zola, you are my half sister." Bobby smiled, which annoyed Tempest. "Even if you don't want anyone to know, everybody does. There's no need to deny it."

She shrugged. "I don't care what anybody thinks."

"Now that you're a big star, you could help me get the family place back. It's mine and my siblings'," Bobby said. "Jonas Callahan stiffed our father out of Dark Diablo. Dad was not in his right mind when he sold it. That land was worth a lot more than what Callahan paid for it."

"Yet he left you none of his money," Tempest said. "I would think that speaks pretty loudly. Anyway, it doesn't explain what you're doing in my house." She glared at Bobby.

Shaman stood stiffly next to her, coiled, ready to

strike. She doubted Bobby knew how much danger he was in.

"I didn't figure my sister would mind." The man shrugged. "You know, if you'd care to speak on our behalf in the lawsuit, testify to the fact that Dad wasn't in his right mind when he sold the land or when he wrote his will, we'd cut you in on the deal."

She crossed her arms. "Just so you know, this is Shaman Phillips. He's working at Dark Diablo."

Bobby turned his full attention to Shaman. "You work for Callahan?"

Shaman didn't reply. Tempest had a feeling silence was deadly, and put her hand in his, trying to let him know he didn't have to worry about protecting her. "Yes, he works for Jonas."

Bobby looked at her with loathing. "So you're in bed with the Callahans."

"Not so much." She heard what sounded like a growl come from Shaman, and squeezed his fingers.

It didn't seem to help. He was like a crouching panther, his tight muscles bunching.

"It never occurred to me before," Bobby said, "but Dad left his money to someone. The will was sealed, so we never knew, but now that I think about it…" He stared at Tempest. "It was you, wasn't it?"

"Why would Bud Taylor leave me a dime?"

"Because he loved your mother, though he would never have married her. She was trash, of course, from the wrong side of town—"

"Then he wouldn't have left her daughter anything." Tempest tried to squeeze Shaman closer, so he'd know he didn't have her permission to go ape-wild on Bobby.

He wanted to, badly—she could feel it. "Bobby, I want you out of my house."

"I've got no place to go," he said.

"Go back to wherever you came from." She glanced around the dark house. "How are you surviving here, anyway?"

"I don't need much. There's some broken furniture, so it's like camping. Besides I'll have plenty of money once the judge forces Callahan to give us what's ours."

"Go," Shaman said. "Go and don't come back. Or you'll deal with me."

"And you're a tough guy, right?" Bobby retorted.

"Something like that," Shaman said, his tone deceptively easy.

Bobby considered him for a long moment. Then he shrugged. "I'll go. But one day, you won't have a job at Dark Diablo. You'll be the first person I fire," he told Shaman. "Hope you don't need your job too bad. And I'll own this house," he told Tempest. "You could have been nice, could have shared with your brother who's down on his luck."

"I could, but I'm not going to," Tempest said. "Get out before I call Sheriff Nance."

Bobby snatched his flashlight off the counter, then sauntered out the door. The kitchen went dark again.

"That was pretty crazy," Shaman said.

Tempest finally shivered. It was nerves, but not good nerves, not like she had before she went on stage. This was more of a bone-deep trembling, from the past smacking her right in the face. "Yeah. It was."

"You trying to scare me off, Cupertino?" Shaman asked, putting his arm around her and walking her to the front door. She could still feel the tension in his body; it radiated from him.

"Maybe," she said. "Is it working?"

"I'm pretty sure it's not," he answered, helping her into his truck. "I don't know that you can scare me off."

He went around to get in the driver's seat, and she suppressed another shiver until he'd climbed in. She quickly locked the doors, and he acted as if he hadn't noticed. "I wanted you to know where I came from, Shaman. I knew you'd understand."

He pulled away from the small, decrepit pile of wooden misery where Tempest had grown up. "I don't know that there's anything to understand. It doesn't matter to me."

"I haven't been back here since I left," she said softly. "And I've never told anybody I dated about my family."

"So this is like a real first date," Shaman said, trying to unload some of the tension.

Yet the tension wouldn't leave her. "I just knew I could tell you, because you're not some rich guy who's never worked a day in your life. You haven't had everything handed to you. I mean, I feel like you could understand."

"Oh, I get it. Because I'm a working stiff." He laughed. "Cupertino, you got a bad-girl fantasy going on? Rich girl meets bad boy?"

"No," she said, annoyed. "I just feel like you and I are a lot alike somehow. That maybe we're from the same place."

"It's okay," Shaman said. "I get what you're saying. And I don't care about your skeletons, beautiful. Now tell me where you want me to take you for our date. A beer is sounding real good to me right now."

"I do not have a bad-girl fantasy, or whatever you said," Tempest said, still inwardly writhing over the skeletons that had popped out unexpectedly from her closet. "I don't have any fantasy at all concerning you," she fibbed.

"We'll have to work on that. I've got plenty of fantasies that have your name on them."

She sniffed. "Really?"

He reached for her hand, kissing her fingers. "Feed me, and maybe I'll show you."

"Turn right at the stoplight. You can get a beer at Shiloh Bill's."

"That's my girl," Shaman said, and Tempest decided maybe the night was looking up. As long as she didn't think about the past, everything was fine.

SHILOH BILL'S WAS A cozy mom-and-pop shop with lots of plants sprucing up the place, and a piano player in the background. Shaman felt himself slowly starting to relax. The whole incident with the vagrant had really teed him off—he couldn't remember the last time he'd wanted to remove a guy's head more.

It was Cupertino. She was driving him mad.

"What are you going to eat?" she asked, looking at him with big, inquiring eyes. He figured most girls wouldn't have wanted to go out in a cap and wearing no makeup, but she hadn't mentioned it. Shaman wondered if she knew how sexy she was, and decided Cupertino was too secure to care, whether she was wearing holey jeans or a ball gown.

"I'm going to have a salad and veggie quesadillas," Shaman said. "Maybe some Oreo pie for dessert."

"Didn't you eat today?" she asked, obviously teasing him.

"Bodyguarding makes me hungry." He reached for the chips in the center of the small table between them in the booth.

"Bodyguarding?" she said, one brow arching.

"Yeah. Do I get extra points for it?"

She laughed. "I can take care of myself, Shaman. And you just like to eat. It has nothing to do with me."

"I wouldn't count on it." He sipped his beer, drinking in Cupertino, feeling relaxation stealing over him like a welcoming hug. "So, I have to ask you something."

She leaned back. "I can't promise to answer."

"This is an easy question. My curious, naturally suspicious mind thinks Bobby's right. Bud Taylor left his money to you."

She looked at him without blinking. "They teach you puzzle solving in the military, or is it a natural talent?"

"Both. I'm right, aren't I?"

She rolled her eyes. "I don't have the money."

He heard the hedge in her answer. "But you did have it."

Her mouth twisted, and he wanted to kiss her soft, sweet lips. "If I did, Phillips, I would have donated it all to charity."

"Would you now?" he said, knowing she'd just answered the question without answering it. A tall, thin waitress with gray hair and penciled eyebrows came over to take their orders, and when she'd left, Shaman looked at Tempest with a grin. "So which charity is your favorite?"

"You might notice that the library has had a major

face-lift," she said, her tone airy. "The structure was sound, but the outside needed work and the inside needed cosmetic renovation. Also, the book selections required serious updating. I think the money must have been appreciated, because your niece spent her summer devouring several shelves of books, and still likes coming here for reading material. Her nana Moira—Chelsea's mother—apparently spent the summer dragging Cat to the library, helping her find her footing among the classics. I deem the project a success, if Cat and Moira think that highly of it."

Shaman whistled. "You're amazing."

"Not really. It wasn't my money, and I didn't need it. The town of Tempest did. I figure no good civilization grows without excellent resources."

He dragged a chip through the salsa. "I guess Bobby would have a fit if he knew."

She shrugged. "That's his personal problem. Anyway, the way the story went, at least the way I heard it from Shinny and Blanche, is that Bud Taylor couldn't stand his kids. Said they were like vultures waiting for him to die, and he didn't understand why they couldn't just go out and make successes of themselves as he had. He didn't believe in leaving them money."

Shaman sighed with appreciation as their orders were placed in front of them. "It's probably true. Everyone should make their own mark in life. Waiting for a handout is a sign of weakness."

"I knew you'd understand," Tempest said. "I admire you for being a self-made man."

He wasn't certain how admirable he really was. "So I take it no one knows your deep, dark secret."

"Not a soul. Well, Bud's lawyer does. But no one else, not even Shinny and Blanche." She dug into the fajitas she'd ordered. "There was no point in telling anyone. Bud wouldn't have wanted anything named after him. I didn't know him very well, but I figure he wasn't that kind of man. And anyway, I don't necessarily believe the rumors are true about him being my dad. I had a father." She stopped, looking faraway for a moment. "I didn't really know him, either. Mom didn't talk about him much."

The salad was delicious, as were the quesadillas, but Shaman suddenly had another topic on his mind. "So, I heard Cat was hinting around about me marrying you."

Tempest blinked and put her fajita down. "She didn't say anything like that to me."

"Oh, boy." Shaman shook his head, realizing his niece had pulled yet another fast one on him. "That little devil."

"Why?" Tempest gazed at him. "Did she tell you she'd talked to me about getting married?"

He nodded, suddenly wishing he'd kept his yap shut. "Cat strikes again."

Tempest laughed and patted his hand, then took a bite of her fajita, unbothered. "I'm leaving tomorrow for New York," she said, stunning him. "Cat's a great girl and I love her, but she isn't the wily meddler she fancies herself to be."

Shaman put his fork down, studying the beautiful blonde across from him. "Were you going to tell me?"

"I…" She looked at him. "I think so."

He closed his eyes for a moment. "Cupertino. You make me crazy."

Her big eyes were round in her face. "I'm not your kind of girl."

He felt as if his fork was lodged in his throat. "No. You're really not."

"You see?" Relief crossed her face. "I was planning to call from New York."

He knew she wouldn't have. "Okay," he said, determined not to make her feel awkward. She had a different life, one that would never include Tempest, New Mexico. "Eat up, since it's your last hometown meal."

He ate as if his stomach wasn't in knots, just to keep the twisting emotions at bay. But the food suddenly tasted like dry crackers and the beer plain water, and he knew he'd fallen a little bit further than he'd meant to.

But he'd always known that in her world, she was the beauty. He was the beast. There really was no bridge between them.

He'd just gotten too caught up in the fantasy.

He was so busy feeling miserable that even though he saw the man exit the booth behind Tempest, his cap tugged low on his face, his gray wool coat pulled up to his neck, Shaman didn't register that Bobby Taylor had been sitting there. Shaman didn't think about it until that night, long after he'd dropped Tempest off at home and he lay sleepless in bed. When he did, his eyes snapped open.

That *had* been Bobby Taylor. And Bobby might have overheard her story.

He might not have.

Chills ran up Shaman's arms.

He should tell her. Then he realized he still didn't have Tempest's cell number. "This is ridiculous," he said, and got up, pulling on his jeans and shoving his feet into his boots. "He probably didn't hear anything. He's a thick-headed moose," Shaman muttered, "and dumb as a rock."

He was trying to comfort himself. Yet worry stabbed at him. He jumped in his truck, driving over to Tempest's almost breaking the speed limit. Her house was dark and her car was gone. Fear snaked through him.

"Looking for Tempest?" a voice asked, and Shaman whirled around.

"Hi, Blanche." He took in a deep, relieved breath, his heartbeat jumping madly. "Yeah, I was."

"She decided to take a flight out to New York tonight." The older woman pulled her shawl more tightly around her. "She said she'd probably stayed here too long."

"Oh." The revelation was painful, more painful than he could have ever imagined. "Okay. Thanks."

"No problem. See you around, Shaman." Blanche unlocked the door to the B and B, going inside.

Shaman drove back to Dark Diablo, his mind whirling with a mad kaleidoscope of images of Cupertino. He replayed their last conversation over and over, trying to make sense of it. Clearly, she'd left because of him. Yet he wondered why. He hadn't even kissed her good-night, preferring to keep everything on a casual basis, the way he knew she wanted it.

He got out of his truck and walked glumly to the farmhouse, wondering why he was so hurt by her departure. Heck, *crushed* was a better word.

Then something crashed against the back of his head, and everything went dark.

Chapter Five

"Shaman, you goober," a female said. "I know you and Gage just love living like a bunch of gophers out here in the middle of nowhere, but I do think sleeping outside is taking it a bit rustic, even for you."

His head pounding, he squinted thinking it was rotten luck that he couldn't have awakened to an angel. September sunshine bore down on him, and even if he hadn't recognized the voice, he would have known the pointy-toed high heels—tulip-pink today—parked next to him.

"Manolo Blahnik," he said.

"What?" His sister bent down next to him. "Get up, Shaman. There is no reason to sleep on the porch. I don't approve of it."

"I know." He groaned, thinking he'd rather continue lying flat-assed on the ground.

"He's been drinking, Xav. Lift him up and drag him in. The neighbors might see, and if not them, then the help will. And they talk."

Holy Christmas, there were no neighbors, and the "help" Kendall was referring to had Sundays off. It was Sunday, Shaman knew, because last night had been his first real date with Tempest, and she'd flown off like a frightened bird.

And then someone had tried to bash in his skull.

Bobby Taylor.

"Crap," Shaman said. "Xav, help me up. Unless you're afraid you'll pull a muscle."

"You're nothing but deadweight," their sister protested. "It would take a horse to drag you up off your back."

"I can take care of him," Xav said, obviously amused. "I thought the military was supposed to toughen you up, dude."

He pulled on one arm and Kendall tugged the other. Shaman made it painfully to his feet, wincing when Kendall gasped.

"You're bleeding!"

"You sure are," Xav observed. "Flapping open back there like a zipper on a woman's dress."

"Thanks," Shaman said, feeling woozy and grumpy and mad as hell that he'd gotten coldcocked. His normal radar that he relied on to keep him alive had definitely been off. "I'm going to kill him."

"Who?" Xav and Kendall asked in unison, as they tried to help him inside.

"Never mind." Shaman didn't want to get into it. He closed his eyes as Kendall moved his head to inspect his nape, then felt a cold cloth being mashed to his skull.

"Is this a woman problem?" she asked. "I don't approve of women problems. I brought Xav out here so you could talk some sense into him."

Shaman sighed. "It doesn't matter."

"Hey," another male voice said, and he opened one eye to see Jonas Callahan coming through the door. "Am I interrupting something? Looked like a puddle of blood on the porch, so I thought Shaman might have shot a bird or a— Why's his head bleeding like a pumpkin losing guts?"

Not his boss, too. The boss that was currently involved in a lawsuit with the man who'd just cleaned Shaman's clock. "I fell," he said, and Kendall said, "Bull-oney."

"Let's get him to the quack shack," Jonas said. "Shaman, I hope this isn't because of Tempest. I stopped in town and talked to Blanche, and she said Cat told her you're in love with a movie star. The only movie star we know is Tempest. I can tell you from experience that you shouldn't be on the bad side of a woman. They use frying pans for more than cooking."

Shaman sighed. "Let's get this done, okay?"

"He's cranky," Kendall said to Jonas. "You have to understand that he might be older than us, but he always had second child syndrome. He couldn't keep up with Gage, and Xav and I were smarter and quicker on our feet. He was never a good patient, because he always milked it for all he could get. It was an attention thing."

"Ha ha," Shaman said. "Either get me stitched up or buzz off."

"Come on," Jonas said. "I'll drive you."

"Good," Kendall said. "We'll follow."

"I kind of like it here," Xav said. "I get why you're out here playing renegade recluse, Shaman."

"No," Kendall said, "I will not lose one more brother to Dark Diablo. Don't even think about it."

Jonas grinned. "Come on, soldier. Let's get you walking wounded."

Shaman was going to kill Bobby Taylor for visiting this on him. All he wanted to do was think about Tempest—and thanks to his well-meaning family and boss, he wasn't going to get one second's peace to do it.

"So," Jonas said, as he drove Shaman back to the farm-house three hours later, "your niece says you're in love with the movie star who was in town."

Shaman's head hurt. He was annoyed, and a bunch of deadener hadn't made the three staples any more fun to bear. "She's not a movie star, and Cat doesn't know everything."

"She is a movie star," Jonas said. "The contract terms were finalized last night. And I don't know about Cat not knowing everything. I should warn you that she's been studying the high art of manipulation and busybody-ing from my aunt Fiona, and there's no more successful teacher alive. You've been warned, friend."

Jonas laughed, his mirth almost contagious if the joke hadn't been on Shaman, which it was. He blinked, try-ing to take in what Jonas had just said. "Tempest didn't say anything to me about the negotiations."

They'd celebrated her big news with beer and fajitas and a trip down haunted house lane. He pondered that a moment, remembering that Tempest hadn't even had a beer—she'd drunk water.

Some celebration.

"So, is Cat right?"

"You just said she knows everything," Shaman snapped.

"So you're in love!" Jonas chuckled, his theory con-firmed. "A movie star and a soldier. Could only write that in Hollywood."

"Not really," Shaman said. "I'm not in love."

"You're not?"

Why would he fall in love with a woman so far out of his league? It would be dumb. "No."

"Oh." Jonas sounded depressed about that. "That's too bad. Sabrina already dragged out the magic wedding dress, in case Tempest wanted to borrow it. Of course, she'll probably want something fabulous by some world-famous designer, but all the same, the ladies in our family are pretty fond of their magic wedding dress. It's all a fairy tale, but it's fun to hear them tell the yarn."

Jonas grinned, but Shaman didn't have a smile in him. He wanted Jonas to stop talking, and he wanted to sit alone with his wounded pride and aching head.

"So, who do you think hit you?" Jonas asked.

"Bobby Taylor," Shaman said, too grumpy to filter.

He felt his boss's stare. "Why do you think that?"

"Just a sneaking thought," Shaman said.

"It doesn't affect what I hired you to do," Jonas said, "and Gage knows all about it. I wasn't trying to keep it a secret. Besides, it's no reason for anyone to try to open your cranium." He shrugged. "When Gage was managing Dark Diablo, Bobby filed the suit. I got a little worried and pulled Gage off the project because I didn't want to build in case the courts decided for the Taylor family. But my brother Sam—he's a crack attorney—said damn the torpedoes and full speed ahead. He told me to get up every building I have my heart set on for Dark Diablo. And there's a lot of building I intend to do. So you need to quit loafing," he finished, his tone jovial.

"I'll do that," Shaman said, "as soon as your enemies quit trying to unhinge my head from my body."

"Good man." Jonas was quite cheerful, but it wasn't his head wearing staples. "I'll give you a few days to rest. And I don't want to hear a word about you handing in your resignation. I fully expect that you can handle Bobby Taylor, even if you did let him sneak up on you. Weren't you supposed to be some kind of sniper or something? I would expect more out of a decorated grunt, to be honest."

Shaman sighed. "Appreciate the vote of confidence."

"No problem," Jonas said. "I hope it works out with the movie star."

"She's not a—" Tempest *was* a movie star, or she was about to be. He was a soldier, and the whole relationship was pretty uneven. Too bad he'd had to get his head whacked to figure it out.

Yet his head didn't hurt nearly as bad as his heart, which was, Shaman thought, even dumber.

"I'm HEADING TO Rancho Diablo to see our niece. I should leave Xav here to keep an eye on you," Kendall said, inspecting the bandage wrapped around his head.

"No," Shaman said. "I'm going to rest. I can't rest when Xav's around. He has the attention span of a flea."

"He's not quite like you remembered," Kendall said. "But we'll leave you here to sulk in peace if you promise to rest."

"I will." Shaman lay on the sofa, his head throbbing. "I'm already resting."

He could hear his sister and brother whispering, conferring about what should be done with him. "Go," he said, tense as all get-out. "I want peace and quiet and a shot of whiskey."

"No whiskey," Kendall said, bossy as always. "You have plenty of drugs the doc gave you."

"Fine." He'd just said it to rile her, give her a reason to worry. "Lights off, please. And get out, sibs."

He heard Kendall and Xav walk out the front door. Shaman's eyes closed, and he sighed with relief.

As soon as he felt better, he was going to have a chat with Mr. Taylor.

THE PHONE RINGING in his pocket felt as if it were splitting his brain into two complete halves. No doubt it was Kendall, calling to check on him. Sighing, Shaman pulled out his cell phone, not recognizing the number. "Yeah?"

"Shaman?" a female said.

"Yep," he answered. "How can I help you?"

"Shaman, it's Tempest."

His eyes snapped open again. "Hi."

"I—I heard what happened. I'm so sorry."

Frowning, he said, "How'd you hear?"

"Cat texted me. And then Kendall called to tell me."

He sat up, wincing as the wound pulled. "Wait. My niece and my sister both have your number?"

"Yes. Of course Cat has my number. We've been talking to each other for months now. Don't you remember she's the reason I came back to Tempest in the first place?"

"Yes, yes," he said impatiently. "I know that. But—"

"And Kendall probably got the number from Cat. Or from whomever she had to bribe to give it to her. You know your sister."

Shaman cleared his throat. "I think my question was more rhetorical. What I meant was, why does everyone have your number except me?"

"You never asked," Tempest said reasonably.

He blinked. "I guess that's true."

"But you have it now," she continued. "Although I know that's probably counterproductive to the status of our relationship."

"What does that mean?"

"Well," she said, "you never wanted a relationship. You made that clear. So you never asked for my number or anything."

"Now look here, Little Red Riding Hood," he said, "you were the one who showed up with your picnic basket whenever you had the urge."

"I knew I'd never get you off the ranch," Tempest said. "You're kind of a hermit. You shocked me when you took me out. Anyway, how's your head?"

"My head is fine." He didn't want to talk about that. "Are you saying that you felt like I didn't want you?"

"I think you're a loner, and if I wanted to bring you food, you'd let me."

"A little more than food, Cupertino," Shaman said. "We should have talked more and—"

"Dined less," Tempest interjected.

"I guess." Shaman rubbed his face. "So listen, I'm glad you called. First, I want to congratulate you. The grapevine works this way, too, you know, and it's let me know you've received some kind of awesome offer that's going to kick your career into overdrive."

"We'll see," Tempest said. "I like the project."

"And, apparently," Shaman said, ticking down his list, "you're crazy about me."

"Did you hear that from the grapevine, too?"

"Yes, I did." It was a tiny fib. The grapevine said he was crazy about her. But there was no reason to give away all the house cards just yet. He wanted to see what she'd say first.

"Funny," Tempest said, "the town grapevine told me that you were walleyed nuts for me."

He grinned in the darkness, glad she couldn't see him. "It's a twisted vine."

"I guess so."

"So now that you're calling me, still pursuing me," Shaman said, "I have a proposal for you. It's not a Hollywood contract type of proposal, but it's one that might interest you."

"I consider all proposals and offers," Tempest said.

It was worth a shot. "About that baby Cat said you wanted."

The silence stretched out. "I might want a child one day."

"Mmm. And if you decide you do, I wouldn't mind letting you try to have that baby with me."

"That's nice to know, soldier."

"I thought you might think so. But here's the hook—"

"There's always a hook with you."

"You have to marry me first. Then we'd practice. I'm not saying I want to get married," Shaman said. "I'm just saying that if you decide the bright lights aren't what you want, and that you want to see if you can handle the heat back here in Tempest, maybe I'll let you get in bed with me again, with that intent in mind."

"Well, that is an offer I'll have to ponder," Tempest said. "Considering I've been chasing you all this time, cowboy, I'm not sure you're ready for a more serious situation."

"You're the one who was going to leave without saying goodbye."

"I figured you wouldn't notice. Then I realized bears get hungry after a long winter's hibernation, and it was the picnic basket you'd miss."

"Exactly," Shaman said. "I don't know what I'm going to do now that you're gone."

"Learn to cook?"

"Doubt it," Shaman replied. "Good night, Cupertino."

"Shaman," Tempest said, "you didn't tell me how you hurt your head."

He wasn't about to, either. There was something going on here, a little forward progress he hadn't been expecting, and he wasn't about to blow it with her feeling guilty. Which she would, if she knew Bobby Taylor had taken a crack at him. "You always warned me about being on roofs," he murmured.

"You're dumb," she said.

"Probably. Thanks for the call, Cupertino."

"'Bye, soldier."

She hung up and Shaman tossed his phone on the coffee table. Yes, there was some forward progress. It still might not go anywhere—right now, she had a little nostalgia, maybe a little fear of the new job, so she was reaching out to the comfortable known.

But if she decided she wanted to be a little more forward still, he'd be right here waiting for her.

THREE WEEKS LATER, Tempest realized that the stomachaches she was having had nothing to do with nerves. Something else was bugging her. She went to the doctor and described her symptoms.

When they asked her to take a pregnancy test, Tempest laughed out loud. "There's no way," she said.

"I know, I know," the nurse said. "The doc can be a crazy old fool sometimes. Humor him and use the cup."

She did, shaking her head. Shaman had been vigilant about using protection. There'd been no wild-and-crazy, passion-blinded moments. The man was serious about not having children. Oh, he talked big, a real good game—but actions spoke louder than words. He practically wrapped up like a mummy before he touched her.

"Guess what?" the nurse said, handing her a tiny white stick with a blue line across it.

Tempest stared at the blue line. "You cannot be serious."

The nurse laughed. "Like I said, the doc's a crazy old fool—crazy like a fox."

"Are you sure my test didn't get mixed up with someone else's?" Tempest's ears seemed to be ringing with chimes or bells or something. Alarm bells.

A pregnancy would mess everything up. Everything.

"You're the only one the doc wanted to test for pregnancy today," the nurse said cheerfully. "Congratulations, you win the prize."

"I guess so." Tempest's mind felt dull and slow. "How can this happen? We used condoms every time. Every single time."

The nurse shook her head. "Not completely foolproof. Good, but not perfect. There's really no perfect birth control, to be honest. Very, very close to perfect, but still, we see this kind of thing all the time. Condoms are about ninety-eight percent effective. You can get dressed now, and we'll make an appointment to have your first prenatal checkup."

"Thank you," Tempest said. She dressed quickly, her brain frozen. Shaman hadn't called her since the night he'd hurt his head. He'd made a big deal out of finally having her number, but then never called.

As her mother always said, if a man was interested, he figured out how to dial a phone. She supposed her mom had known what she was talking about, if she'd gotten Bud Taylor to use the phone. Bud had been a total recluse. The only time he'd left the house was to broker a deal, see his lawyer, grab a bite in town. Mostly he had his groceries brought to him at the farmhouse.

In that, he and Shaman were a lot alike.

Tempest squeezed her eyes shut for an instant, then put her hand on her stomach, feeling a thrill that she was going to be a mother. Secretly, this was her dream come true.

"It doesn't matter about the cowboy soldier," she said. "You've got me. Welcome to the world, little baby."

What difference did it make if history might be repeating itself just a bit?

SHAMAN RUBBED HIS EYES when he saw the Land Rover parked outside the farmhouse. It wasn't Kendall's; she was in Diablo with Cat and Gage, and generally trying to keep her twin, Xav, away from the "gold digger," a topic Shaman had heard more about than he ever wanted. The only other person he knew who drove one of those cars was Tempest.

He strolled up to the house, looking for his surprise visitor.

Tempest sat on the porch in the swing, looking so beautiful Shaman thought he could wait on her forever, if she'd just show up every once in a while to make him feel the things only she made him feel.

It was almost worth the wait.

"Hi," she said.

"They give you a break from filming, or whatever it is you do?"

Tempest didn't smile at him, didn't get up. "I quit the production." Her face seemed strained as she said it.

"Sorry to hear that. Didn't you like it?"

"I liked it a lot. Turn around and take off your hat, please."

She wanted to see his busted noggin. He wasn't going to acquiesce. "That's not one of your better come-on lines, Cupertino."

"Probably not," she said. "Let me see the damage."

"No damage," he said. "Barely a scratch."

A truck rumbling up the drive caught Shaman's attention. "Is that Jonas's truck?"

"I think so—"

"Does he have Cat with him?"

Tempest stood. "It looks like he might."

"This is great! You did not see me." He raced inside, grabbed a water gun and ran back outside.

"Shaman!" Tempest exclaimed.

"Shh," he said, hurrying around the side of the house. He squatted low, hidden from view. "Don't rat me out."

"You can't squirt your niece!"

"I can. And I will. She has it coming to her."

"You're an unnatural uncle," Tempest said under her

breath, just loud enough so he could hear. "I don't think I ever saw this side of you."

"Hi, Tempest!" Cat exclaimed, rushing from the truck to hug her. "I didn't know you were back in town!"

"Hi, honey." She lowered her voice, as if whispering to someone stage right. "Your uncle is at the side of the house, ready to douse you with his water gun."

"Okay. I'll get him." Cat went running back to Jonas. "Uncle Shaman's hiding on the side of the house, about to ambush me with his soaker gun. Distract him, Uncle Jonas."

"Easy to do." He walked toward Tempest, who smiled at him.

"Hello, Tempest," Jonas said. "So how's the big city treating you?"

She watched as Cat got her water blaster from the truck, sneaking around the opposite side of the house so she could trail Shaman. Tempest grinned. "The big city's nice."

Jonas nodded. "Any truth to the rumor that you're expecting a baby?"

Chapter Six

"What?" Tempest said, stunned.

"What?" Shaman exclaimed—and then yelled as Cat fired. It sounded like a direct hit; Shaman's roar brought an explosion of giggles from a delighted Cat. Tempest couldn't help laughing, proud of Cat for getting to Shaman before he could get to her.

Fairly drenched and a bit wild-eyed, Shaman came around the house to stare at Tempest. His eyes went to her stomach, then to her face. He glanced at Jonas for confirmation. "Did I hear him right?"

His shirt was soaking wet, and water dripped from his hair. Cat had certainly won this battle. Tempest smiled. "Jonas was just trying to draw you off guard, Shaman. It was sneaky, but it worked."

Cat came out of hiding, giggling. "Uncle Shaman, you should see your face!"

"Did I spill some beans?" Jonas asked. "Cat mentioned something about a baby, but I might have misunderstood."

"Yes, I am expecting a baby," Tempest said, sighing.

Shaman looked shell-shocked, and Jonas laughed out loud. "Congratulations," he said, kissing her on the cheek.

"Am *I* going to be a father?" Shaman asked.

She nodded, silently watching him. Tempest didn't think she'd ever seen him look more handsome. It was the look of incredulousness on his face that stole her heart.

"This isn't good," Shaman said. "You're not the marrying kind."

"Uh, Cat, honey, why don't we go check out Candy and see how Shaman's doing with training my beautiful mustang?" Jonas suggested.

"Okay." Cat happily followed him with her water gun.

"I might be the marrying kind one day," Tempest said.

"You were supposed to marry me and then we were going to go for baby. This is all backward." Shaman shook his head. "The baby was the hook."

"The hook?"

"To get you to marry me. Now you've got the baby, you don't need me." Shaman sopped some water off his face with his sleeve. "Marry me, Cupertino."

"Aren't you going to ask me how it happened?" she said. "Aren't you the slightest bit curious? You were so careful."

"I *know* how it happened," Shaman declared. "Tempest, I spent every second I could making love to you. Condoms are not one hundred percent effective." He sighed. "I should have told you no."

"Told me no?" Tempest was outraged.

He nodded. "I should have. The thing was, I couldn't resist you. No man could."

"Well." She leaned back, not exactly mollified. "I don't know about that. Anyway, you're stalling. Let me see your stitches."

"They took them out. There's nothing to see."

"That'll teach you to climb up on roofs."

"Probably not," he said. "I don't suppose I can talk you into marrying me when we only had one date."

"Does seem a bit premature."

"So does having a baby."

Tempest shrugged. "True. You know, babies grow up to be little girls toting water pistols."

"Are we having a girl?"

Tempest smiled. "Do you really want to know?"

He came and sat beside her. "You don't even know, Cupertino. It's too soon."

"But will you want to know?"

He sighed. "Either way, the baby'll probably learn practical jokes from the Callahans before it's taller than my knee. Callahans are equal opportunity pranksters. You see what they've done for Cat."

Tempest flicked his forearm with her finger. "I didn't say the baby was going to be raised around here."

He leaned back on his elbows, a raffish, handsome man not worried about anything in his world. "The baby will be raised, Cupertino, wherever I have a job. So go ahead and stew about that. You've got nine months to give me plenty of lip about it."

She didn't have to. She didn't know Shaman well, but she'd seen him in action—and she'd known he was going to feel that way about his child.

It was one of the things she really, really liked about him.

THE EVENING WAS BEAUTIFUL and crisp, and Shaman would have taken the time to enjoy the expansive quiet of Dark Diablo, but his twin siblings were staring at him, wanting him to play referee. It wasn't going to do them any good, because there was no playbook as far as those two were concerned.

"I'm staying," Xav said. "Jonas offered me a job, and I'm going to take it."

Kendall sighed dramatically. Cupertino had left, leaving Shaman in a mess of conflicted emotions. Jonas had returned home with Cat, so Shaman had been sitting on the porch swing, staring up at the half-moon, trying to figure out what he was going to do about Tempest.

Then his sister and brother had driven up, their disagreement apparent as they walked up to the porch.

"Do something, Shaman," Kendall pleaded. "I don't know what it is about this place. You guys get out here and you lose touch with reality."

Shaman grinned at his brother. "Liked Rancho Diablo, did you?"

"I never realized there could be so much silence," Xav said. "No fax machines, no ringing phones, nothing. This is what I need in my life. I heard a coyote last night." His face held a look of ecstasy. "The sound of the rat race is pretty deafening, bro."

"What about the girlfriend?" Kendall demanded, her tone a little desperate.

He shrugged. "Shaman doesn't have one. He's not married. And he's fine. Gage only just got married, and he's four years older than me. I've reconsidered this marriage thing. I don't want to jump too soon."

"Well, about me having a girlfriend—" Shaman began.

"What about Mom? Who's going to take care of her?"

Shaman and Xav both stared at Kendall. Even Shaman thought she was stretching the pity party.

"Millicent will be fine. She will outlive us all," Xav said, "and that's a good thing. You and Mom can run Gil Phillips, Inc., which will make you both happy. And I," he said with a contented sigh, "am going to learn to build things, use my muscles and commune with owls. That's what Jonas said. Spirit owls."

"Oh, no," Kendall moaned. "Look what you've done!" she told Shaman.

He shrugged. "You know, sis, he's got a point."

"He does not!"

"I do," Xav said. "I'm going to cede all my shares in the company over to you, sis."

"Moratorium on life plans, Xav," Shaman said, "before your twin's head pops off. Go easy, bro."

"Xav, you and I have been running the company together for years," Kendall said. "How would I do it all by myself?"

He kissed his sister on the forehead, drawing a frown from her.

Shaman grinned. "Kendall, there has never been anything in life you couldn't face on your own."

"That's right," Xav said. "Beautiful, smart—Gil Phillips in female form."

"That's just great," Kendall said. "What if *I* decide to just take a midlife detour? Go off the deep end? Commune with spirit owls?" Her hands were on her hips.

"We'd sell the company," Shaman said, and Kendall gasped. "Anyway, I'm having a baby. Let's go celebrate my fatherhood and Xav's decision to commune with nature."

"A baby?" Xav and Kendall echoed, sounding like the twins they were.

"Apparently," Shaman said, feeling really good about everything except how he was going to get Tempest to marry him. That would be a puzzle, a holy grail in itself. He couldn't worry about that right now, though; he felt like he was walking on air and nothing could bring him down.

"Wow," Kendall said. "With the big blonde?"

"I prefer to think of Tempest as delicate. Elegant. Just right."

"Whatever," Kendall said. "I guess your kid will always be chosen first for basketball."

He laughed and shook from his hair the last drops of water that their wily niece had doused him with. "I am almost the happiest man on the planet."

"You see what happens out here. Happiness," Xav said to Kendall, and she groaned.

"Moratorium, bro," Shaman said, but Xav had figured it out. Life was better away from The Family, Inc.

Now Shaman just had to figure out how to convince Cupertino that she needed him in her very independent life. "I'm going into town to try to drag Tempest out to dinner. Wanna ride shotgun?" he asked Xav. "I'll introduce you around, since you think you might want to make this your home for a while."

"Sure," he replied. "I'm game."

"Lovely," Kendall said. "Guess I'll come along and try to remind you two that life is always better with money. And a Nordstrom nearby. At least a Macy's."

The brothers laughed, then picked her up and carted

her to Shaman's truck. Just like old days, Shaman thought. Them against the world.

"I DON'T THINK I've ever eaten in a place called Cactus Max's," Kendall said as they seated themselves in a booth. "Quaint. When's the skyscraper going to be here?"

"Easy, sis," Shaman said. "That's the woman who's having your niece or nephew."

"Yeah," Kendall said. "So tell me what you decided to do about the wild-to-wed fiancée, Xav, while we're waiting on Tempest."

"I phoned her and told her I thought we should call it off," Xav said, and Shaman checked his brother's face for any signs of regret. There was none. "She was a gold digger, like you said, Kendall."

"I knew you'd figure it out," Kendall stated. "Women can be tricky." She slid a glance at Shaman, who grinned at her.

"Uh-uh," he said. "You're not running Tempest out of my life like you ran Xav's woman out of his."

"I did no such thing," she said haughtily. "Xav decided he loves the rural countryside more than he loves a trollop. Or his family, apparently."

"Hi," Tempest said, sitting down next to Shaman, interrupting Kendall's complaining.

The dark, circular booth they were in was well placed and away from the late-day sunlight streaming in the windows, just right for the mood Shaman was in. He didn't want people staring at them.

"Am I really going to be an aunt?" his sister demanded.

Tempest smiled. "Seems like it."

Kendall looked as if she wanted to say something rude, then shook her head. "I guess only a pretty wonderful woman could get my brother to settle down."

"I don't want to settle him down," Tempest said.

Shaman gazed at her. "Well, you have, sweetie. Get used to it."

"Because of a baby?" she said. "Come on, Shaman. I have no father to take a shotgun to you, to make certain you marry me in the town square by sundown."

Shaman nodded, and accepted a menu from Blanche when she came by to take their orders. "We'll talk about wedding plans later. Blanche, do you ever not work?"

She put glasses of water in front of everybody. "Oh, the ice cream shop is all Shinny's deal. I just hang around in there with him because I love him. This is my real job. What can I get you folks?"

They all ordered, then Shaman took a deep breath. "Cupertino, awkward as this may be, you're going to have to marry me," he said. "Believe it or not, you were meant to be my wife."

"Not if she doesn't want to be," Kendall stated.

"Yeah," Tempest said, glancing at his sister with a glare of suspicion. "A baby does not mean marriage. I have contracts I can't get out of, Shaman, and dreams of my own. I don't want to live in this backwater."

"You see?" Kendall told Xav. "Most people can't wait to get away from this place."

"Oh, he'll be happy here," Tempest declared. "It's the perfect place for a single man avoiding matrimony and commitments."

"Oh, boy," Shaman said, signaling for a bottle of wine. "I think those are words likely to start a debate."

"No," Tempest said. "Ask Kendall if she'd like to live in Tempest."

"Absolutely not," Kendall said, horrified. "I'm always delighted that my sojourns here are brief."

"I like it," Xav said, his tone sure. "Gage is going to teach me how to breed horses."

"What's to learn? You just need a syringe and a quick hand," his twin said with disgust. "Tempest, please tell my brothers that they are being blinded by the lure of the unknown."

"I don't know," Tempest said thoughtfully, staring Kendall down. "This town has a lot of charm."

She frowned back at her. "That's not what you just said."

Shaman grinned, realizing Tempest was trying to get under Kendall's skin, and was succeeding. His sister didn't even realize that she was needling her.

"Heaven on earth," Tempest said, and Kendall let out an unladylike snort that Shaman thought he'd never heard from his refined sister.

"All right, girls," he said. "Let's change the subject."

Blanche brought over the wine. Kendall was in no mood to be good company. "I don't see what you two have in common, besides a baby," she said, deciding to do a little needling of her own.

Tempest met Shaman's gaze. His stomach tightened, just looking at her. "You make me crazy for you," he told her.

"More wine," Kendall said, and Xav laughed.

"One day Kendall's going to fall in love, and you and I will have our revenge, bro," he said to Shaman.

Shaman surprised everyone by leaning over to kiss Tempest. Then he took her hand in his. "Marry me."

Tempest's eyes went huge in her face as she stared at him.

"Come on," Shaman said. "Aunt Kendall is dying to be your maid of honor. Uncle Xav can be my best man. We'll do it nice and quiet in Las Vegas."

"All right," Tempest said, shocking him.

He grinned. "I knew you couldn't resist me."

"But," she said, and Shaman held his breath, "I want Cat to be my junior bridesmaid."

"Deal," Shaman declared. "I can probably work that out with my brother. Everybody on board?"

He glanced at his sister and brother.

"I am," Xav said, high-fiving Shaman.

"I guess," Kendall said ungraciously, and Shaman laughed.

"You sound like Mom when she's not happy with us," he said, and Kendall stiffened.

"Welcome to the family, Tempest," Kendall said, her tone much sweeter. She'd obviously been stung by his comment. "It will be so wonderful to have an actress in the family. Maybe you could even give us one of these wonderful paintings of you for the main house."

Tempest blinked. Shaman glanced at her, then his sister. "What paintings?"

Kendall looked at him, frowning. "The huge ones at the four corners of Cactus Max's. Didn't you notice? They're life-size, Shaman, not hard to spot."

He looked around with a sinking heart. Tempest was on every wall of Cactus Max's, in various stages of costume. How had he missed it? Obviously, all he could see was her in the flesh.

He forced himself to look around, taking in the town of Tempest's tribute to their favorite daughter. She was stunningly beautiful in the oil renderings, and in that moment, Shaman realized that he and Tempest were, as Kendall had noted, as different as night and day. "Wow," he said.

Next to him, Tempest squirmed a little. "That's not real life."

"Looks real to me." He didn't know what else to say. He hadn't figured on falling in love with a movie star when he was fighting in the dirt-laden, dangerous war zones he'd lived in for the past ten years. He looked at Tempest, who stared back, her normally lively face a little pale and drawn. She didn't look all that happy, and he wanted her to be. "Sure you want to get married?"

Tempest nodded slowly.

He ran a thumb along her bottom lip. "It's going to be all right," he told her, feeling her uncertainty. And he just hoped like hell that he was right.

Chapter Seven

They flew to Las Vegas the next night with Cat. Gage came along, of course, to see his brother marry Tempest. Rafe Callahan flew the Callahan jet, which meant that Fiona could go, too, as well as Chelsea, Gage's wife.

Fortunately, Tempest had a white pantsuit she could wear. Kendall had asked—nicely—if her pale peach skirt and jacket would be all right, pairing that with cream high heels. Cat wore a darling white dress, tea-length, with white flats.

But it was Shaman who held Tempest's gaze. Dress jeans, dark jacket, leather belt, black dress boots made him look dangerous and sexy, and it was all she could do to make herself believe they were actually going to be married.

She and Shaman stepped up to the altar, with Cat beside them, holding Tempest's white rose bouquet as the rings were exchanged. Tempest's heart thundered as she looked into his dark eyes. She couldn't believe this amazing man was going to be her husband, and the father of her child.

The ceremony was over so quickly it didn't feel much like a wedding. She'd barely said "I do" when Shaman gave her a brief kiss, and then Xav and Gage were congratulating her.

Her new husband was very quiet. Withdrawn. He'd barely kissed her at the altar of the little Las Vegas chapel.

"Back on the jet, family," Shaman said, after tipping the Elvis minister and his pink-haired wife, who'd played a harp for their ceremony.

"No wedding dinner?" Kendall asked.

"Are you hungry?" Shaman asked.

"I'm not," she said, "but your wife and niece might be."

He turned to look at them. "Do you want to get something to eat?"

"I'm not hungry," Tempest said, partly because it was true and partly because she could tell Shaman wasn't in the mood for a wedding dinner.

"I'm not, either," Cat said. "I sneaked some brown sugar cookies on board, so I'm fine."

"I've got leftover roast and veggies at home," Fiona said. "We could have a meal there."

"I'd like that," Tempest said, and Shaman nodded.

They left and got in the jet, more like a tired soccer team than a wedding party. Tempest tried to tell herself she wasn't disappointed—she'd known that this wedding was all about the baby.

SHAMAN COULDN'T BELIEVE he was married. The gold ring on his finger was proof, though. The weirdest thing was that he now had a gorgeous wife sleeping in his bedroom.

Tempest was all his—for now.

He wandered out to the den, not wanting to bother

her. He was still missing a chunk of hair in the back, so he kept his hat on all the time. He didn't want Tempest to see how badly he'd been injured.

But he couldn't hide it—or his fears—forever.

"Hey," she said, walking out to join him in the small den. Moonlight spilled into the room, surrounding her with gentle light. She wore a white nightgown that reached her ankles, and if she knew it was a bit see-through from the moonlight, she'd probably be embarrassed. He admired her body, the perfection of it, and the knowledge that his child grew inside her. "Isn't it traditional for newlyweds to sleep together on their wedding night?"

"You looked like you needed rest."

"I'm rested now, if you want to join me."

It was an invitation he thought it best to turn down. "Go back to bed. I'll join you in a bit."

"I'm not going without you."

He raised a brow. "Is that so?"

"Yes." She drifted over to him and took his hand. "Don't be scared. I don't bite."

He laughed. "Even if you did, it wouldn't necessarily be a bad thing."

Feeling his body anticipate the pleasure of being with her, he let her pull him down the hall toward the bedroom. "Wouldn't it be better for the baby if we waited until after?"

"After?"

"After it's born."

Tempest unbuttoned his shirt. "Tough guy, are you afraid?"

He was, a little. "I don't want to hurt you."

"Then get in bed with me."

She unbuttoned his jeans, and his vow to leave his new wife alone until after the baby was born swiftly ebbed away. He caught Tempest's hands in his, stilling them. "There's something we should talk about first."

"I agree. You start." She pulled him into bed with her, which he realized was a ploy to get his mind off his talking points and onto what she was trying to get him to think about—her fabulously soft, welcoming body.

She was about to succeed.

"All right." He caught her hands, kissing her fingers. "You can't stay here."

Tempest stilled, then sat up, pushing her long blond hair away from her face. "What are you talking about?"

He'd been more in control of things before she'd sat up. Now her breasts were at eye level, and his resolve was definitely weakening. "You're going to have to stay somewhere else."

"I'm staying right here, soldier. That's what wives do. They stay with their husbands."

"You're not." He pushed her back on the pillows, unable to resist her any longer.

"Hang on a minute. Catch me up on this, Shaman, because I don't think I follow you." Tempest slid out from under his kisses. He let her go, reluctantly.

"I have bad timing," he said with a sigh.

"You clearly have something on your mind," she countered.

He took a deep breath. "I would feel more comfortable if you stay at Shinny and Blanche's B and B for now."

Tempest looked mad. Really mad. He couldn't blame her, but he also didn't want to tell her the reason he felt so strongly. But Bobby might be around, and maybe next time he would attack Tempest. Shaman was certain Taylor was the man in the next booth the night she had mentioned she'd inherited Taylor's money and then donated it to the library, among other places.

The man had a score to settle, and Shaman didn't want him settling it with Tempest.

"No, thanks," she said.

"No, thanks, what?"

"I'm staying right here with you."

She crossed her arms. He recognized stubbornness, and normally would have welcomed her determination to be with him. "It's not a good idea."

She flipped on the bedside lamp and glared at him. "Why? Because you think Bobby Taylor laid open your head?"

Okay, so she didn't want him trying to hide things from her. He got that. "Who told you?"

"Kendall. Who do you think?" Tempest said, clearly annoyed. "She wants you to do a better job protecting yourself, so she told me. And she said she knew you didn't want me to know, but since her unborn niece or nephew was involved, she figured it was better to be safe than sorry. Kendall isn't self-motivated all the time."

"I know." Shaman sighed. "Yes, that's exactly why. I don't trust him. I don't know that he did it, but I'm not going to give him a chance to get to you."

"I would be flattered by your desire to protect me if you'd allowed me to be in on the decision, considering it's my family that's causing the trouble," Tempest pointed out.

He had to concede the point. "I see where you're going with that. But your enemy is my enemy, as they say."

"I'm not leaving you, Shaman," Tempest said. "At least not until our marriage is over."

He rubbed at the nape of his neck. "I have to stay here to keep an eye on Jonas's place. That's part of my job, besides renovating this joint. But I really would feel better if you weren't here."

"Tough." She snapped off the lamp and pulled him down next to her. "I'm not used to taking orders, soldier."

"I see that." He couldn't help being amused. It was hard to stay angry, anyway. Her hair smelled like flowers and she'd wrapped her body next to his, laying her head on his shoulder.

Damn. There was nothing else he could do.

He surrendered.

Chapter Eight

"So I hope last night wasn't an indication that arguing is your favorite form of foreplay," Tempest said the next morning when she brought a glass of water out to Shaman. There were no crews today—Sunday was their day off—so he was working Candy, Jonas's beloved and (according to her husband) bad-tempered mustang. "Because if verbal sparring gets you hot, you and I may have a slight problem. I go for the silent types. Men of action."

Shaman glanced at her. "I've been called the strong, silent type."

"Good." She hitched herself up onto a corral rail to watch him train Candy. "Kendall called."

He held the lead loosely as he guided the mustang in a circle. "Yeah?"

"She says to expect a visitor around noon."

"Why didn't she call me?"

"She said your phone was off. It worried her. She wants you to start carrying your phone from now on, and leave it on."

"I'm surrounded by opinionated women." He grinned.

"Don't you forget it." Tempest blew him a kiss and slid off the rail. There was a lot she had to do.

"Cupertino."

She looked at him. "Yes?"

"We never finished our discussion."

Her husband was not a fast learner. "Yes, we did."

"I'd like to revisit that discussion. It would be safer if you didn't stay here."

"I'm married to a man who has a bagful of guns, seems to have supersonic hearing, and doesn't play well with others. I feel safer here than anywhere else."

She went inside to grab some things. Shinny and Blanche would want to hear all about the wedding.

Tempest's cell phone rang and she reached for it, answering as she looked out the window at her husband working Candy.

It was her agent.

"They're willing to hold production over until after you have the baby. Some financing fell through and it'll take time to line up more, so they are opting to wait on you," Jack Collins said.

Candy bucked suddenly, and Tempest's breath caught. Shaman calmed the skittish horse, then maneuvered her into doing just what he wanted: nice, wide circles around him.

They were all going in circles.

"I may not want to do the film," Tempest said.

"It's a huge career boost," Jack said. "Production will only be about five months."

"I know." There was nothing keeping her here. Once the baby was born, everything would change.

She could go back to Tuscany, to the villa she loved.

But not as much as she loved being with Shaman.

"All right," she said. "But the baby comes with me."

"I'll work it out." Jack sighed. "You're giving me gray hair."

"I got married last night," Tempest said.

"Oh." Jack hesitated. "Congratulations."

"Thanks." She knew Jack was thinking about how her marriage changed her marketability. She didn't care if it did.

"A baby and a marriage. Lots of changes."

"The time was right. Goodbye, Jack."

"'Bye."

She hung up as Shaman came in, dirty and sweaty.

He looked sexy as all get-out.

"That was my agent on the phone. I have a job lined up for after the baby is born. That should solve a lot of things."

Shaman washed up at the sink. "If you say so."

She went into the kitchen and handed him a paper towel. "Toss those grubby clothes in the washer, and I'll put the soap in and turn it on for you."

He laughed. "Too dirty for you?"

She sniffed. "Yes."

"This is what I'm like all the time, Cupertino."

She looked at him. "If you're trying to scare me off, it's not going to work."

He ran a paper towel around the back of his neck. "So who is our first visitor?"

"Kendall didn't want me to tell you."

"But you're not married to Kendall."

"So I should do what you tell me to do?" Tempest shrugged. "Your mother."

"My mother?" He looked at her. "Not possible."

Tempest grabbed her purse. "I'm going into town to

see Shinny and Blanche. They're the only people I know who are telling the truth when they say they like looking at wedding photos."

Shaman followed her. "Don't you want to meet my mother?"

She glanced at him. "Not really."

"Isn't that a bit unusual for a bride? Aren't you supposed to want to suck up to my mother and get on her good side?"

"No," Tempest said. "This is a short-term marriage, and Kendall says your mom's coming to bend your ear about your responsibilities. I think I'll leave you two alone. Kendall said you and your mom could probably use some time to hash things out. I'm making myself scarce."

He caught her hand. "You know, that's the second time you've reminded me that we're getting a divorce after the baby is born. Are you trying to tell me something?"

She tugged her hand away. "Yes. I'm trying to tell you that we're getting a divorce after—"

"I got that part." He caught her again, pulling her against him. "I may not let you go."

She looked into his dark eyes. "I have a contract."

"You have a marriage contract, too, Cupertino. You may have to decide." He kissed her, and she giggled.

"You smell like horse." She gave him a slight push and brushed off her white top and blue jeans. "A limo just pulled up outside. Anyone you know?"

He sighed. "It's Millicent. My mother."

Tempest glanced at him, then out the window, surprised. "Your mother has a limo?"

"A few of them. Come say hello. If Kendall told you

Mom's a bit of a dragon, let me just say my sister exaggerates sometimes."

Tempest followed Shaman, if for no other reason than curiosity. "Kendall said your mother's a sweetheart, and that you can be a grouch around her. I was supposed to tell you to mind your manners."

Shaman walked toward the limo. "As I said, Kendall exaggerates. Hello, Mother."

Tempest watched as a wheelchair was brought out of the limo by a uniformed attendant. Shaman gently helped his mother ease into it. He kissed her on the cheek, and the elderly woman gazed up at him reproachfully.

"You're gone for four years, and you don't come home regularly to see your mother?" she demanded. "I have to get in the car and come all the way out here to God knows where I am, to find you?"

Shaman took the handles of the wheelchair, rolling her toward Tempest. "Mother, I'd like you to meet my wife. This is Tempest Thornbury. Tempest, this is my mother, Millicent."

Millicent sniffed. "I hope you won't regret marrying my rude son, Tempest. Welcome to the family."

"Thank you, Millicent." She smiled and shook her new mother-in-law's hand, glancing at Shaman, who had the grace to look a bit sheepish.

"Take me inside before I roast," Millicent said. "And tell Fitzgerald where he can rest. It's not easy driving out here, you know. It's like the center of the earth. And now you've caught Xav up in your madness. At least I can count on Kendall. She'll never leave me," the woman added with a dramatic sigh.

"We didn't leave you. We left The Family, Inc." Shaman rolled his mother around the back so he could wheel her into the kitchen. "Fitzgerald, make yourself comfortable. There's plenty of stuff to graze on, thanks to Tempest," he said to his mother's driver.

Millicent looked at Tempest. "I suppose a wedding gift is in order, even though I wasn't invited to my son's wedding."

"And a baby gift," Shaman said, "if you're in a shopping mood, Mom."

She glanced at Tempest's stomach. "You always were determined to follow in Gage's footsteps, Shaman." She glanced toward the kitchen, where her driver was enjoying a cool glass of tea and some fruit. "Fitzgerald, fix me a toddy, please."

"Certainly, madam." He pulled a flask from his suit pocket, preparing to utilize the emergency container.

"That's not necessary, uh, Fitzgerald." Tempest glanced at Shaman. "Shaman, please fix your mother a drink. Our cabinet is stocked with anything she might like."

"Is it?" Shaman went to peer into the unit. "Wow. You are a woman after my own heart." He looked back at Tempest. "None of this for you, though."

She shook her head, pleased that she'd surprised Shaman. "Not a drop. Millicent, how do you like your—"

"Whiskey. Neat. No fanfare. I've gotten used to drinking out of Fitzgerald's flask," Millicent said. "I'm spending more time on the road now that my sons have decided to shirk their duties."

Tempest smiled at her complaining. "We don't need a wedding gift, but thank you for offering, Millicent."

Their visitor sipped the whiskey Shaman handed her,

eyeing Tempest. "Go ahead and ask me for a big gift, because I'm about to ask Shaman if he was smart enough to get you to sign a prenup. As beautiful as you are, I'm thinking he didn't." She glared at Shaman. "Did you?"

"Hell, no." He glanced at Tempest. "I don't even own the roof over my head. She's welcome to half my guns if she wants them."

"A big gift," Tempest said thoughtfully. "I like big gifts, Millicent."

"Surprise me," Millicent said. "When Chelsea married Gage, I gave them matching saddles and all the accoutrements. It's what they wanted. And it cost me a pretty penny." She sighed. "So go ahead, tell me you want matching boots and hats, or whatever. Because then I've got papers for you to sign."

"How'd you know we'd gotten married? Kendall?" Shaman asked.

Millicent waved a hand, and Fitzgerald dutifully pulled a *USA TODAY* from his coat pocket, handing it to Shaman. There was a picture of Tempest and an announcement that she'd gotten married to a soldier of fortune who'd swept her off her feet. "'The wedding was very romantic,'" Shaman read. "'The happy pair is now honeymooning in a private location before Ms. Thornbury returns to her impending role as Lady—'"

"Stop," Tempest said. "I'm going to kill my agent."

"Oh," Shaman said. "I didn't factor agents into the equation."

He looked at her, as did Millicent and Fitzgerald, and Tempest felt ridiculous standing here in this tiny house with her other world magnifying their differences.

"Hey, I realize nothing's ever really real in Hollywood, but I have a couple of quibbles," Shaman said.

"You are a master quibbler," his mother interjected.

"It wasn't a romantic wedding," Shaman stated.

"No, it wasn't. But Jack's a bit of a... He exaggerates." Tempest was terribly embarrassed. It all sounded so fake, when these people were used to lives that were a bit more realistic.

"It wasn't romantic?" Millicent said. "Guess I didn't miss much then. Fitzgerald, top me off, please."

"And I wasn't and am not a soldier of fortune," Shaman said.

Tempest flushed. "I know that. I'm sure Jack thought it sounded exotic."

"Oh, I realize he was covering the fact that you had a quickie wedding. He was definitely building onto your glamorous résumé." Shaman shrugged and handed the paper back to Fitzgerald. "Anyway, Mother, as you can see, there's no need for a prenup."

Millicent sighed. "You haven't told her, have you?"

Tempest stared at Shaman. "Told me what?"

"Nothing." He looked at Millicent. "Not now, Mother."

"I see." She shook her head. "I don't understand why you just don't—"

"My life is here," Shaman said. "The Family, Inc., is not mine."

"It is," Millicent said. "Here are the papers, and a pen, Tempest."

"Mother," Shaman said, practically growling.

"Oh, for heaven's sake. Give me that pen," Tempest said. "Goodness, Shaman, your mother came all the way out here to have these papers signed. It's not that big a deal." She flung her signature across the bottom of the pages, one after another, without reading them.

She handed the document back. "Happy?"

"Delighted." Millicent nodded. "Thank you."

"Okay. If that's it, Mother," Shaman said, "then maybe you'd best—"

"I want my wedding gift," Tempest said, "if you're about to run your mother off, which I don't think you should do, Shaman. She has a right to look out for you."

"What would you like, my dear?" Millicent asked.

"A very large donation to the local elementary school," Tempest said. "Folks are having to be a little more careful with their donations, and I hear the town budget is smaller these days. An anonymous donation, unless you'd prefer to make it in your name."

Millicent blinked. "I didn't think you'd surprise me, but you have."

Tempest smiled. "Would you like to see the wedding pictures, Millicent?" She pulled out the album she was taking to Shinny and Blanche.

Millicent grabbed the album from her, glanced through the pages eagerly, then looked up at Shaman. "You got married by an Elvis impersonator?" she demanded. "That seems a bit beneath a Phillips."

Shaman looked at her driver. "How about a Millicent special for me, too, Fitzgerald?"

The man nodded and made the drink.

"What is going on?" Millicent demanded. "You two are not acting like newlyweds. This feels more like a business transaction."

"That's because it kind of is," Tempest said. "We're only staying married until after the baby is born."

Shaman groaned. "Time-out. This is not a business transaction, Tempest. It's a baby."

"Actually," she said, "it's two babies."

"What?" Shaman felt a bit light-headed. His mother glanced at him, concerned. "Twins?"

Tempest nodded. "Guess I'm just full of surprises."

"You certainly are," Millicent said, her tone somewhat admiring. "I had my four one at a time. Couldn't have handled them any faster." She glared at Shaman. "Can't handle them now."

Stunned, he shook his head, feeling as if he'd been knocked to his knees. "Tempest, we have to talk."

"Guess that's my cue," Millicent said ruefully. "Ah, well, no one ever wants the mother-in-law around, anyway."

"I do," Tempest said quickly. "We're going to have dinner with Cat and Gage. Please join us, Millicent."

Shaman's mother sniffed. "She has manners," she told her son. "I accept. Gratefully. Fitzgerald is starving. I can hear his stomach rumbling across the room."

"Yes, ma'am," her driver said.

"Oh, hell." Shaman poured another whiskey and handed it to Fitzgerald. "You're off duty for the night. We might as well all toast the good news my wife has sprung on me. Mother? Dinner?"

"I thought you'd never ask," Millicent said.

"I wasn't going to," Shaman said.

"I know," she replied. "Tempest, you may wheel me to the car. We can all ride together."

"Here's to your good fortune, sir," Fitzgerald said, "and to you, Mrs. Phillips." He raised his glass, and Shaman nodded.

"It is good fortune. Come on, wife. My mother wants you to do the honors. I think she likes you better than me."

"It's all your fault," Tempest said. "Mothers just want to be treated kindly. Kendall says you have all these barriers, that you can't just relax—"

"That's good," Shaman interrupted, thinking he wasn't certain how his wife had managed to tame his driven sister and his thick-skinned mother, but she had. "Everyone into the land yacht. No more beating up on me."

Millicent sniffed. "You bring it on yourself. You're more like your father than you realize."

Shaman winced. "I hope not." He'd been running from the old man's shadow almost all his life.

If he was anything like Gil Phillips, he wouldn't have won a woman like Tempest. The thought comforted him as he watched his beautiful wife push his mother's wheelchair toward the limo.

Then he remembered he hadn't won Tempest, and she was carrying his twins, and life should be amazing. He should feel like he was on top of the world.

He would be—when she quit insisting their marriage had an expiration date.

Chapter Nine

"Cactus Max's?" Shaman asked Tempest, but she shook her head as he drove toward town.

He remembered all the portraits and wondered if she didn't want Millicent to see them.

"If it's all the same," Millicent said, "I'd love to go to Cactus Max's. My darling granddaughter, Cat, tells me there are pictures of you so big in there, Tempest, that they look like they belong in a museum."

Tempest made what Shaman thought sounded like a groan.

"We know you're a celeb, babe," he told her.

"I don't think it's the way to make a good impression on one's mother-in-law."

"On the contrary," Millicent said. "Gives me hope that maybe the two of you will be able to keep a roof over your heads. And my grandchildren's cribs."

"We're going to be fine," Shaman said. "I make enough to keep food on the table."

"You could make more if you came back home and took your rightful place—"

"I'm going to slide the window up between us, Mother," Shaman said, and Millicent said, "Oh, never mind. I won't say another word. Although I am going to invite Tempest to come home with me, Shaman. Just so you know."

"I'd love to visit your home," Tempest said, before Shaman could say *don't even think about it, Mom.*

"You really don't want to," he insisted, pulling in front of Cactus Max's.

"Oh, but I do. Cat says it's like a palace."

Now it was his turn to groan. "Now who's going to get the wrong impression?"

"Not me," Millicent said. "I just came along to bring a smile to everyone's stiff upper lips."

"And you're succeeding," Tempest told her.

Shaman shook his head. "I'm surrounded by females whose greatest joy is to torture me."

"Exactly. And look who has arrived," Tempest said in delight, as Cat and Gage and Chelsea met them at the entrance. "How did you get here so quickly?" she asked, watching Cat fling her arms around her grandmother.

"Your texts were pretty clear," Gage said. "Hello, Mother." He hugged his mom a bit more warmly than Shaman had, Tempest noticed. Shaman hadn't quite made the transition from wayward son to returning prodigal.

She understood those emotions. As much as Tempest had loved her, her mother hadn't been a giving, maternal person. Bud Taylor hadn't been a man she would have ever wanted to be close to, and she barely remembered her father. Sometimes Tempest thought she only remembered the memories her mother had shared of happier times, over too soon. It could be hard to be close to people when you hadn't experienced close-knit bonds in your life, and she knew Shaman hadn't felt close to his mother or father.

Millicent didn't seem all that bad. Perhaps she'd mellowed over the years Shaman had been deployed. Tempest didn't hold it against Millicent for wanting her to sign an agreement.

But it seemed as if Shaman wasn't happy at the moment. "Hey," she said, as they seated themselves at a big, round table. "Are you in shock?"

"I'm processing as fast as I can, doll." He shook his head. "Are you still going to want to sleep in my bed? Because I kind of dig being with you."

She laughed at his question. "Is that what's bugging you? You're afraid having twins makes me off-limits?"

"Can we order?" Millicent demanded. "You two can whisper later."

Shaman snapped open the menu. "I just don't know where I stand. It makes me crazy."

"You are crazy," Gage told his brother. "Thank you for taking him off our hands," he said to Tempest. "He was the problem child."

"I don't doubt it." Tempest grinned at her husband. "Split veggie fajitas with me?"

Chelsea smiled at Tempest. "I'm so glad you're my sister-in-law now. Someone who understands the joys of living with a vegetarian."

Millicent sighed. "Shaman, will you please go rescue Fitzgerald from that woman?"

They all looked in surprise at Millicent, then across the room. Fitzgerald sat under a TV in the bar, enjoying a tall drink and a pretty redhead who was chatting him up. For an elderly gentleman, Shaman thought, Fitzgerald was managing just fine.

"He looks happy enough to me. Fitzgerald can take care of himself, Mother."

Tempest glanced at her mother-in-law, then turned her gaze to Shaman. "It wouldn't hurt to shoo off his new friend, do you think, Shaman?"

He looked at her, surprised. "A man likes to have the attention of a pretty woman sometimes, Tempest. She's not hurting anything."

His wife gave him a small kick under the table and he blinked, realizing that she was trying to tell him something. He wasn't certain what message he was supposed to be receiving but he sighed and got up. "Can't a man have a little companionship?"

"No!" Chelsea and Millicent and Tempest said at once.

"I kind of hate to do this to the guy," Shaman said. "It's probably the first attention he's had in years. I know I was a lonely man until you came into my life, Tempest. Thing about it is, if we weren't pregnant, I'd be sitting over there with Fitzgerald."

"I assure you," Millicent said drily, "that Fitzgerald is not suffering from a lack of attention. I'd wheel my chair over there to help him out, but I have two sons at this table who can do the honors for their mother. But I can do it myself if I must."

"Oh," Shaman said, finally getting it. "Excuse me, ladies."

He did his duty, noting that Fitzgerald seemed pleased with the intervention. Shaman tried diligently to process the fact that his mother was involved with her chauffeur, then decided it wasn't any of his business. "All right," he said, returning to the table. "The coast is clear. Fitzgerald is out of commission, and the lady will have to go find another gentleman to play with."

Cat looked at him with big, round eyes. "Wow, Uncle Shaman. Don't you know I'm not supposed to hear things like that? I'm even supposed to believe that babies are brought in by magic storks in the night."

Shaman grinned at her. "That's right, sweetie. You just keep on believing it, too."

"Because if any boy ever tries to convince you that you should kiss him—" Gage began, but his daughter raised a hand to silence him.

"Dad, it's uncool to bring it up all the time. I get it. Boys are icky."

"That's right," Gage agreed.

"That's right," Chelsea said, "for now."

"Boys are icky," Tempest said, "until you find the right one."

Everyone looked at her. Millicent stared, Chelsea stared, Gage stared, and Shaman smirked at his family, whose gazes then locked on him. "Well, of course I'm Mr. Right. What did you think? That Tempest is the kind of woman who has to settle for subpar?"

"Oh, brother," Gage said.

Cat smiled at her uncle. "You are awesome, Uncle Shaman. That's exactly what I told Tempest when I said she needed to come meet you. That's when you were living in Italy, Tempest, remember?"

Shaman looked at his wife. "You came all the way back here for a blind date my niece arranged?"

He thought it was darling that Tempest blushed. "Are you going to order dinner or not?" she demanded.

He laughed. "I had no idea how much fun family

could be." Then he leaned over and kissed her on the cheek, deciding to quit worrying about their marriage for the moment.

He wanted her so much. It was an ache that never seemed to subside. Shaman ruminated on this, in a hazy glow of falling-in-love, until he realized that Bobby Taylor sat in a corner of the bar, watching them. The man was sizing them up, letting Shaman know he was aware of every move he made.

Shaman's not-completely-healed wound started to itch and burn at the back of his head, and he instinctively reached out for Tempest's hand. She was starting to mean the world to him—she was becoming his world—and the surge of undeniable killing rage he remembered from war flowed into him, burning with intensity. He recoiled from the memory, surprised—but only for a moment.

He'd protect her and his family at all costs.

He walked over to the man at the bar.

"Evening," Taylor said, nodding to Shaman. "How's the head?"

Shaman felt his blood boil. He had family here tonight, and wasn't in the mood to have the discussion with Taylor he really wanted to have. "I'm assuming you decided your little job on my skull was necessary because of your sister."

Taylor shrugged. "Didn't say I did it, Phillips. Heard about it in town. I don't know who clocked you."

"Sure you don't." Shaman wondered if Taylor was certifiable or just working things through in his own vengeful way. "Saying it was you, why would you think busting open my grapefruit would get you even with Tempest?"

"Again, not saying I did anything to you. Why would I? But I could see getting her attention through the man she's having a baby with." Bobby glanced across the room at Tempest, who was watching them, her face frozen with an emotion that looked a lot like fear. "You know, Tempest never had anyone in her life who really loved her before."

"I don't believe this is about love." Shaman stared at Taylor, holding back the urge to wring his neck here and now. "It's about something else."

"She stole from me. She stole from our family. My siblings and me should have had what was ours. She came along, and I guess Dad figured she was the right person to leave the whole thing to. I don't understand that."

"It doesn't matter what Bud Taylor did. It was his money, his land. Tempest had nothing to do with his decision."

"I see she hasn't told you everything," Taylor said. "The woman you call Tempest—my half sister, Zola—told our father that if he didn't recognize her as his legal daughter, she'd sue him to take a paternity test."

Shaman winced. "That doesn't sound like Tempest."

"Ask her." Bobby lifted his glass of whiskey. "It was all about the money."

"She makes enough to live all right." Shaman didn't know that for certain—they'd never discussed money—but everything he'd heard about Tempest seemed to indicate she did just fine on her own.

"You'd best talk to your wife. She spent enough time with Pop at the end of his life to turn his head, make him rewrite his will. And suddenly, all of us were out in the cold. How do you expect us to feel?"

Shaman wasn't about to share that Tempest said she'd donated all the money. Taylor had to know; he'd been sitting in the booth that night when she had told her story. "I know this is a dumb question, but if your father built his stake from nothing, why don't you do the same?"

"You don't get it, do you? You're just a farmhand, so you wouldn't," Taylor said dismissively. "Look, it's biblical. The birthright should go to the child it belongs to, not be stolen away by an impostor."

Shaman swallowed, trying to understand Taylor's world view. "I don't really care about the beef between you and your sister. I want you to leave her alone. She's my wife now, and I will protect her and my family. And if that means taking you out, I'll do that. I won't lose any sleep over it, either."

"I know." Taylor put his glass on the counter. "Tough guy."

Gage came to stand beside him, overhearing the last comment. "Tough guys. Plural."

Taylor got up from the barstool. "Tell Zola her brother wants his due."

"I'll tell her nothing, and you won't, either," Shaman said. "That's how this works. You say one word to Tempest and I beat the stuffing out of you."

"And then I beat more stuffing out of you," Gage said. "It will not be pleasant."

"Yeah, I'm scared," Taylor said. "But which one of us has a scar under his Stetson?" He sauntered from the bar, raising a hand to Tempest in a meaningful wave as he left.

"I'm going to kill him," Shaman said.

"No, you're not," Gage told his brother. "He'll step in it eventually, and we'll get him locked up legally."

"I'm worried about Tempest." Cold snakes of fear wound through Shaman's stomach.

"Yeah. She should probably come stay at Rancho Diablo. There's a lot of companionship and stuff out there, and lots of babies. She'd probably enjoy having a bunch of women to gab with, anyway."

"Maybe that's a good idea." They headed back to the table.

"What was that all about?" Millicent demanded. "You two looked like you were about to engage in fisticuffs. Can I point out that I'm in a wheelchair? I can't knock your heads together as I once did."

"Yeah," Cat said, "Dad, you looked like a hulking bear. And Uncle Shaman was all puffed up like one of Uncle Jonas's peacocks."

Shaman looked at Tempest, seeing her pale face. "Hey, this is supposed to be a party. Let's eat, everyone," he said, as the food was served.

"What was that all about?" she whispered as he took his seat next to her.

"Nothing," Shaman said, "nothing at all."

Of course, if she ever learned that her half brother really had taken a whack at him, and Shaman hadn't told her the truth, all bets were off. He had a feeling Tempest wasn't the kind of woman who took being fibbed to very well. Still, he couldn't be honest—how could a man tell his wife that her brother had in fact decked him?

He was afraid for her. He didn't want her having any contact with Taylor. The thing about Tempest was that she'd confront Bobby, if she felt she needed to.

"So what do you think about going to see Kendall and Xav at Rancho Diablo?" Shaman asked his wife.

"I'm going out there tonight," Millicent said. "Tempest can ride in the limo with me and Cat, if she likes."

"Oh. I'll stay with Shaman," she said. "Thank you, though. I may drive out tomorrow to visit."

Shaman completely lost his appetite. He kept seeing Taylor's sweaty face. "I'd rather you go with Mom."

"Yeah, Aunt Tempest, come with us! Nana Fiona's knitting you some baby booties. And there's almost always gingerbread."

Tempest smiled, but looked at Shaman. "I think newlyweds should stay together."

"I'll drive out tomorrow for a bit, after the crews are done at Dark Diablo," Shaman said.

"I'll wait to ride with you, then." Tempest picked up her fajita, dismissing the topic.

Shaman and Gage glanced at each other. Gage shrugged, and Shaman decided to drop the subject. For the moment.

But something was going to have to be done.

"SHAMAN," Tempest said when they were alone that night, after Millicent and everyone had piled in either the limo or Gage's truck to head back to Rancho Diablo. "We've been married less than forty-eight hours and you're trying to send me away." She ran her hands down his chest. Something had Shaman tense, taut, strung tight. She wanted him to relax and go back to being the man she'd known this summer.

The man who'd loved her every minute he could.

He moved her hands away from his chest. "Tempest,

I don't think it would come as a shock to you if I said that we don't know each other very well. We don't have a lot to build on."

She blinked. "Oh, I see."

He took a step back, his face creased with unhappiness. "Maybe we jumped into things a bit fast."

She shook her head. "It's more than that. It's something else."

"I wanted to give you my name." He looked straight into her eyes and she saw shadows there, shadows she'd never noticed before. "I wanted to give my children my name."

"Stop," she said. "You're not telling the truth. You once told me I had to be honest, but you're not doing the same."

"All right. I don't see where this can go. You know we wouldn't have gotten married, and wouldn't even be together, if you weren't pregnant. You'd be on a stage somewhere, or traveling the world."

She felt pain like she'd never known. "This is pride talking."

He shook his head. "When you've lived in the places I've lived, you know the difference between ego and truth. We should stick to our original agreement, and not pretend there's anything more."

"I don't believe you. I don't believe one word you're saying." Tempest picked up her purse. "Maybe you do, but I don't."

He watched her as she walked to the door. "You know, Shaman, I know a little something about acting. I know something about make-believe. And right now, I know you're acting." She gave him a sad smile.

"I don't know why you're pretending you don't care about me, but I know you do."

"Where are you going?"

She shrugged. "What do you care?" she said, and walked out the door, already wishing she was in bed with Shaman, letting him hold her the way she knew he wanted badly to do.

Chapter Ten

By May, Shaman was devastated. No one would tell him anything about Tempest. Even Cat didn't seem to know her whereabouts. He knew full well that the twins should have been born by now.

He'd blown it.

There was no question he'd made a major strategic error. Such poor thinking would have cost him dearly in the war zone. "The problem," he told Candy, "was that I wanted so badly to protect her that I ran off the only thing that made me feel redeemed. She was the other part of my soul, but I never told her that."

Candy pranced in an almost perfect circle, her coat glossy and black. It had taken him months to gentle her, train her, mold her into the beauty she was now. The barn had gone up, a new bunkhouse had been constructed, and Dark Diablo was no longer a lonely dot on the road between nowhere and somewhere. There was a new roof on the main house. Jonas was so pleased with the changes at his ranch that he'd given Shaman a monster raise and offered him long-term employment. Jonas wanted a big house built out here, in the style of the family home in Rancho Diablo, and he wanted Shaman to oversee the project.

Shaman was considering the offer. He still had the horse program to get off the ground, though he now had six good horses in the barn. It was a start.

Someone else could take over the job. He felt as if he was waiting, hoping, for something that was never going to happen. But now he knew: Cupertino was never coming back.

The flip side of this realization was the one silver lining: Bobby Taylor no longer worried him. The man floated around town, telling everyone who would lend an ear that Tempest had stolen from him. No one listened. Everyone knew the truth.

Shaman kept a gun loaded in the farmhouse, but he knew Bobby's one cowardly act wasn't likely to be repeated. Taylor had really been after Tempest, his rage stoked by overhearing their conversation in the restaurant that night. Shaman knew Bobby was still living in the old Cupertino shack where Zola had grown up.

But Tempest had left Zola behind long ago, and Shaman didn't figure it mattered whether Bobby camped out in the falling-down rattrap.

His mother made the donation to Tempest Elementary School, anonymously, as Tempest had asked, even when Shaman told her that his marriage had been, as she'd noted, a business transaction.

"A promise is a promise," Millicent told him, and sent the check. "Nothing's keeping you here now. Fitzgerald and I are getting married, and I want to retire. So it's time for you to focus on Gil Phillips, Inc."

He kissed her. "Congratulations. When's the wedding?"

"In a month. I'm waiting for a special wedding suit I ordered from New York."

Shaman was happy for his mother. She was completely different from the woman who'd raised them, and who'd been Gil Phillips's wife. "You deserve happiness."

"We all do," she'd snapped back, in true Millicent style. "You'd be happy if you weren't so stubborn."

But he was stubborn. It was perhaps his finest trait. Stubborn enough to stay in the military after he'd been hit by a sniper, stubborn enough to drag to safety a man in the line of fire, stubborn enough to run off a wife he loved like crazy in order to protect his children and her.

"I could have kept Tempest here," he told Candy, "or I could have moved away with her. The thing was, this is her home. She was ready to come home." But Bobby had been determined to take his revenge on his sister.

There was nothing that could be done about Taylor's desire for vengeance. The money he sought was gone, the lawsuit decided in Jonas Callahan's favor.

"Candy, I'll miss you. When I first laid eyes on you, I thought Jonas had brought me a bag of bones, mean bones, to train. I thought he was nuts. But you know, he's not as dumb as he looks. You turned out well, pretty lady."

He led her into the state-of-the-art barn, not letting any of the hands take her from him. He rinsed her off with a hose, then swept the water from her coat with a plastic sweat scraper. He ran a gentle comb through her mane, then took a towel to thoroughly dry her, though he didn't really need to. The warmer weather would have done so, but he wanted to spend a few last moments with her.

When he was finished, he gave her a final pat. He walked to the small farmhouse, picked up his gun bag and his duffel, loaded his truck and drove away from Dark Diablo, his heart in a lot worse shape than when he'd first arrived almost a year ago.

SHAMAN PULLED INTO Hell's Colony, sudden memories washing over him at the sight of his family home rising up on the Texas horizon. The large buildings always seemed to overwhelm the landscape, a colossal group of white structures sprawled across the land Gil Phillips had amassed.

Shaman pulled his truck into the drive, and a uniformed attendant came to greet him. "Welcome home, Shaman," he said. "I'll park this for you. Miss Millicent is waiting for you in the great room."

Shaman looked at the valet. "New procedure?"

"At some point in the last ten years, sir, I believe Miss Millicent instituted valeting as part of our job concerning the vehicle fleet. It's nice to have employment, sir."

This was true. Shaman knew it as well as anyone. He grimaced. "All right." He turned over his keys, and walked inside the contemporary-style mansion with a sense of déjà vu and apprehension all wrapped up together. Though he hadn't been home in years, he well remembered where the great room was. Usually it was a silent place, all white, with only a black piano to relieve the coolness. He shivered, feeling a chill despite the May heat.

Millicent wasn't in the room. He ambled over to a window, staring out, wondering if the house had always been so quiet when he and Gage and Xav and Kendall were growing up. He didn't remember. Mainly they'd stayed outside, trying to distance themselves from their father.

Shaman had been something of a nerd, finding an outbuilding to hole up in and read. He'd graduated vale-dictorian, so the studying hadn't gone to waste. Kendall had been more interested in riding, and Xav followed anything his twin did. Gage had mainly raised hell on the rodeo circuit when he could slip away, something he'd managed to do fairly often.

Shaman had always wished he was more like his big brother. A little more of a rebel, a little less of a nerd.

"Hi." He heard a voice behind him, and he turned.

Tempest stood there, just as beautiful as he remem-bered, bringing color to the white room and the austere atmosphere, and most of all, his soul. There was a giant white pram next to her, and Shaman knew his children were in it.

He strode over to look inside, his heart in his throat. Two little wrapped bundles lay sleeping inside. One baby had a thumb in its mouth, the other had a hand on its sib-ling. "Hi," he said to Tempest, and then to the babies, feeling tears push into his eyes. "Hey, there, little peo-ple." He reached a finger into the pram to touch their soft clothes. "They're beautiful. What are their names?"

"Shaman Jonas and Gage Xavier Phillips," Tempest answered.

His gaze jumped to her face. "Both boys?"

She nodded.

He looked back into the pram, staggered. His sons. He was the father of two little boys. "I can't believe it," he said, hardly able to take in the new lives that were part of him. "They're amazing." He glanced back up at Tempest, wanting so badly to put his arms around her and hold her tight, celebrating this moment. "When were they born?"

"About three weeks ago." She was obviously delighted, a proud mother. He thought she glowed with something he'd never seen before, a mixture of happiness and confidence and sheer joy. "I was confined to bed for the last few months, but everything went absolutely fine with the birth."

He couldn't help it; he pulled her to him. "I'm sorry I missed it."

She moved out of his arms after a moment. "I have it all on video, though I doubt you'll want to watch it. Men don't want to see that sort of pain."

He looked back in the pram. "I'm not that strong, to be honest." He knew he couldn't bear to see Tempest in pain. "I'm pretty sure I'm one of those guys who's happier knowing less than more about how babies arrive."

"Like Cat said, magic storks."

He nodded, looking at Tempest sheepishly. "Yeah." Then it hit him. "I didn't expect to see you here."

She shrugged. "Your mother invited me."

"I'm glad." He was thankful, for once, for his mother's overbearing fortitude in all matters. "I bet she is loving having grandchildren in her house."

"The boys were born in the hospital in Hell's Colony. Your mother insisted I stay here when I was put on bed rest." Tempest smiled down at her babies. "I've become very fond of Millicent. You'd be surprised what a doting grandmother she is."

Tempest gave him a questioning glance that held some annoyance. "You forgot to mention how your family lives. This place doesn't exactly square with how you presented yourself to me. Now I see why Millicent wanted me to sign those papers."

"I didn't leave anything out. This isn't my home. Hasn't been in years." He stared at her, torn between gazing at his babies and drinking in the sight of his wife after all the months apart. "I've missed you," he finally said.

She looked at him, remaining silent.

"I would never have guessed you were here." Understatement of the year—he was shocked she and the boys were right here, under his nose. Trust his mother and Kendall to pull a fast one on him.

"I went to New York to do some work. Millicent kept in touch with me, as did Shinny and Blanche. They became quite communicative with each other. Apparently, everyone felt it was best for me to be here to have the babies. When the doctor advised bed rest, I needed to go somewhere. You didn't want me in Tempest," she said, shrugging, "so I came here."

"It's not that I didn't want you."

She glanced away. "It's hard to imagine you growing up here."

"It was never a good fit, probably. Maybe more for Xav and Kendall, because they were the youngest. And because they were twins, they had each other. Gage and I relied on each other, but two years is still a big difference. We were lonely, not being with other kids our ages."

She looked at him. "I can see that. Strangely, I like it here. I think this part of Texas is beautiful. Kind of outback and lonely, maybe. I can understand why you wouldn't be happy here, though."

He didn't want to talk about it. "And now? What happens now?"

"Millicent wants me to stay. She and Fitzgerald want less to do with the day-to-day operations of The Family, Inc. Kendall can handle most, but she wants an assistant. I was asked to take the job, and I've accepted." She smiled at her children sleeping in the big white pram. "It will allow me to be with the babies, which is all I really want to do right now. I'm taking an indefinite hiatus from acting. Though I wouldn't tell my agent, it's probably forever."

Shaman couldn't believe how beautiful Tempest was. Being a mother agreed with her in a way he could never have understood, probably never would. He didn't want to talk about anything but her. "I didn't handle things well between us."

"No. You didn't."

"I'm not good with relationships."

He supposed she had likely figured that out herself.

"So why are you here? Obviously not to see me or the babies."

"I came home to… I don't know why." Why? He'd finished his job. He'd gotten wandering feet.

He'd missed the hell out of her, mostly.

"I came home because it was time."

"Going to work in the family business?"

"Millicent said she could use some help."

Tempest nodded. "It's true. It was good to see you, Shaman. I have to take the babies upstairs to the day nursery. They'll wake up soon and want to eat."

His throat tightened. He wished she'd stay a little longer. "Thanks for…letting me see the babies. They're beautiful, Tempest. I'm the happiest man in the world." *Almost.* He wanted to tell her she was the most beautiful woman in the world, and that he'd missed her more than he could put into words. Yet he knew she didn't want to hear that. She was still upset with him, and he couldn't blame her.

He understood the feeling of abandonment. It wasn't the world's most fun emotion, and essentially, Tempest felt he'd abandoned her.

He didn't know how to fix it.

She smiled at him—barely—and wheeled the pram down the hall. He heard the elevator ding, and the doors close. He shut his eyes, his heart burning, wishing so much that things were different between them. He'd missed the boys' birth.

I'm really a father. I have sons. I had no idea it would feel this in-my-face glorious. It's like Christmas and birthday and every other holiday rolled together.

It was all the best feelings he'd ever experienced melded into one overwhelming haze of joy.

"It's about time you came home."

Shaman opened his eyes to see Millicent parked in front of him. He bent down to kiss her on the forehead. "Obviously. Why didn't you tell me Tempest was here?"

His mother gave him an innocent look. "It wasn't my place to butt in. She said you didn't want her staying with you. It hurt her feelings, I suppose. She said a wife belonged with her husband, even if it was a short-term situation." Millicent glared at him. "Probably you handled things in a rather ham-handed manner, but I'm sure you had your reasons."

"I did."

"Heavens knows your father wasn't exactly the silver-tongued prince, either." She sighed. "I thought it was best to keep her here where we could help her. Truthfully, I figured you'd be here before now. I keep forgetting how stubborn you are."

"Not stubborn." Okay, he was stubborn like the old man. He appreciated his mother's forbearance on the topic.

"Anyway, Tempest made us promise that if she stayed here, we wouldn't breathe a word to you." Millicent shrugged. "I figured you'd be mad at first when you found out, but then you'd realize we did our best in a bad situation, which, I might add, you created."

"I'm not mad. I'm grateful. Though I would have loved to be at my sons' birth."

Millicent sniffed. "I hear there's a video, which I will not be viewing. However, you may find it of interest." She rolled her wheelchair down the hall. "Good to have you home. See Tempest about your duties tomorrow."

He blinked, then caught up with his mother. "See Tempest about my duties?"

Millicent gave him her most innocent look yet. "Tempest is learning the ropes of Gil Phillips. As an actress, she seems to do well with representing us in a positive fashion. Our clients respond well to her. She's more outgoing than you are. She's more like Kendall, to be honest." Millicent smiled. "And Tempest keeps the schedules. We're much more organized now than we ever were. Kendall loves having her here."

"Exactly how long has Tempest been in Hell's Colony?"

"About five months." Millicent wheeled her chair into the elevator, leaving Shaman stunned. "See you at dinner. You might recall that it's served promptly at six o'clock."

He was aghast. All this time his wife had been so close and he hadn't known. He'd worried about her, wondered about her, missed her.

This was going to change. Right now.

A butler appeared. "I'm to show you to your room."

"Show me to Tempest's room, please."

The man looked uncomfortable. "Miss Tempest doesn't have a room in the main house."

"Great. Which of the outbuildings is it?"

"I'm not at liberty to say, sir."

"I'll just stay right here, then." He wasn't about to be in a room that didn't contain his children. Not now.

"Sir?"

"I'm not moving from this spot until someone tells me where my wife and children live."

"Very good, sir." The butler withdrew, and Shaman seated himself on the white sofa. He closed his eyes, feeling drained from the drive, and yet filled with wonder about his children.

Thirty minutes later, Kendall shook him awake. "Hey, big brother. This is no place to snooze."

"Take me to Tempest."

"She doesn't want you staying with her."

"Fine. But I want to know where my children are."

Kendall sighed and sat down next to Shaman. "You hurt Tempest when you decided you didn't want her living with you. Now you're on her turf, and she says she wants to keep the same arrangements."

"Look," Shaman said, "here's the deal. You know her brother took a bat or something to my skull. Bobby Taylor was really angry that Tempest had given away the family fortune, and he was looking for revenge. He started with me, and was trying to get me out of the way so he could get to Tempest. He's still living in the rat-trap where she grew up." Shaman took a deep breath. "I didn't send her away. I wanted her and my children safe."

Kendall nodded. "*I* know all this. The problem is you didn't have time for your marriage to grow. She doesn't want you forcing a relationship now that doesn't exist. Not that she knows whether you would want to or not, but it's clear she'll leave, Shaman, if she feels she's going to be bothered all the time. And to be honest, it wasn't easy getting her to agree to live here with us. We were frantic she'd go back to Tuscany or London or something, and we'd never see the babies. So Mom and I are pretty much insisting that you live here on Tempest's terms, now that you've finally decided to come home."

"Jeez." He didn't know if he could live within five hundred yards of her and never see her. Never touch his children.

"She's going to give you a schedule of visitation for the boys," Kendall said. "I hope you can understand her position."

"I guess." His heart was breaking.

"I'm so sorry, brother," Kendall said softly. "I know you're a prince. Give her some time, and let her figure it out, too. I think it's the best plan. We don't want her leaving. And maybe if you go slowly, things will work out. At least I hope so." She looked at him with sympathy.

"I hate always being the beast in everyone's book."

Kendall laid her head on his shoulder. "In mine you're the handsome prince, brother."

He dropped his head back against the wall and put an arm around his sister. "Thanks."

"Don't let it swell your ego."

"No danger of that." He smiled. "It's just nice to hear it every once in a while."

Kendall didn't say anything for a minute, and Shaman told himself he wasn't going to let anything destroy his big day of learning he was a dad. Maybe he'd failed as a husband, but he was going to be a great father. Nobody got the chance he'd been given and screwed it up.

He was so blessed.

"Hey, how's Millicent, anyway?"

"In love." Kendall stood, smoothing down her fuchsia skirt. "It's great to see her and Fitzgerald so happy." Then his sister gave him a mock glare. "Of course, she is not happy with you one bit."

"Do continue the litany of female displeasure."

Kendall rolled her eyes. "Mom's not happy because Xav's not here."

"He's a big boy. He can make his own choices. Besides, isn't it better that he isn't with the gold digger?"

His sister shrugged. "The problem is that Jonas Callahan hired him. Mother may not forgive you for that."

"She already knew this. Xav has been out at Rancho Diablo for a few months now."

Tempest rolled in the pram, stopping when she saw Shaman and Kendall talking. "Am I interrupting?"

"No," they both said.

Shaman was glad Tempest had come back. "My sister's filling me in on the news."

"Not much news," Kendall said, "except that Xav has taken over your old job at Dark Diablo. Mother's fit to be tied. She was hoping he'd get this ranching thing out of his system. She blames it all on you."

"Oh." Tempest looked at Shaman. "That's too bad."

He shrugged. "Xav stayed here when Gage and I left. Can't blame him for wanting to branch out now."

"I don't blame him, and neither does Mother. She blames you." Kendall grinned at him. "She's a bit irrational when it comes to her boys."

His sister peered into the pram at her sleeping nephews. "They remind me of me and Xav. Being a twin is great."

She left, and Tempest studied Shaman.

"I could have handled our first meeting better, Shaman," she said.

"It's fine."

She didn't know if it was fine or not. He'd stunned her by appearing at his family's home. She knew very well this was not his favorite place on earth. It would have been nice to have a bit of warning that he was coming.

Millicent had been shocked when Shaman called to say he was planning to come hang around the old homestead. They'd figured he didn't plan to ever darken the doorstep again.

Tempest had had a terrible case of nerves. And then when she'd seen him, it was as if all the old feelings, all the burning attraction, all the giddy pleasure, had captured her again.

There was no reason to allow herself to feel anything but professional toward Shaman. It had always been a business transaction.

"Still, these are your sons. You're welcome to see them anytime you want."

"I plan on it. I plan on it often."

She folded her lips. "I just came back to say that the

babies are in the upstairs nursery while I work in the morning. I usually take them back to the guesthouse in the afternoon so they can eat, and then we take a siesta."

"Thank you for letting me know the routine."

She wondered about his real reason for returning, since he hadn't known she was here. "Are you planning on staying long?"

"Maybe."

If he was going to keep up the one-liners, she wasn't going to hold up both ends of the conversation. "Good to see you," she said, and turned to leave. At the door, she nearly bumped into Kendall, who came streaking back into the room to throw herself in Shaman's arms.

"Sheriff Nance just called from Tempest," she said, looking very un-Kendall-like as she clung to her brother. "Xav's had an accident at Dark Diablo. I think he's hurt badly!"

"I'll go," Shaman said. "Don't worry. Everything will be fine. Don't tell Mother just yet, until I find out what's going on."

Tempest held her breath. Shaman picked up the duffel he hadn't even unpacked, then kissed his sister on the top of her head. "Don't worry," he repeated. "I'm sure it will be fine." He kissed his babies, then nodded at Tempest.

And left.

Kendall flew to the door to watch her brother go. She waved, and then closed the door, sobbing into a tissue. For once, Kendall-the-perfect was completely beside herself, her eye makeup running, her face creased with misery.

"Oh, Kendall," Tempest said. "I am so sorry! Come sit

down. It's going to be all right." She desperately hoped she was right.

She guided Kendall to the sofa, found her a fresh tissue. "Sheriff Nance is wonderful. He'll make certain everything is fine until Shaman gets there. And I bet Gage is already at the hospital with Xav." She hoped it was nothing serious. Surely it was some slight accident. Anything could happen on a ranch.

Kendall shook her head, trying to compose herself. "I don't know. Sheriff Nance didn't say much. Something about Xav having an injury similar to Shaman's—"

She gasped, and stared at her.

"What?" Tempest asked. "What is it?"

Kendall shook her head. "Nothing. I'm sure it's nothing."

Tempest grabbed her arm. "Tell me! You looked like you'd just seen a ghost!"

"I'm not supposed to tell you," Kendall said. "I'm going to go lie down for a few minutes before dinner. I just want Shaman to hurry, and—"

Tempest didn't let go of her. Something strange had crossed Kendall's face, and it had to do with her. "*Tell me.*"

"Shaman will kill me for this," Kendall said, "but he didn't hit his head falling off the roof." She took a deep breath. "Your brother ambushed him. Shaman lost a lot of blood. I don't know what would have happened if Xav and I hadn't found him."

Tempest turned ice-cold. Shaman hadn't wanted to tell her the truth about Bobby. He'd hidden the scar until his hair had grown out, and he'd never answered her questions honestly. Then he'd told her he wanted her to live somewhere else. She'd been hurt, thinking he didn't want her around. "And you think Bobby might have done the same thing to Xav...."

"I don't know. I've said too much!" Kendall got up from the sofa. Tempest could see her hands trembling. "I'm just so scared," she said, her voice shaking. "Xav's my twin, my best friend. I..." She looked at Tempest, then murmured, "Please excuse me," and disappeared down the hall.

Stunned, Tempest stared at the pram where her twins lay sleeping. Her brother had attacked Shaman, and he hadn't wanted her to know. He'd tried to protect her. And she'd left, taking her heartbreak elsewhere instead of staying to work it out.

Maybe Xav's accident didn't involve Bobby. Maybe he'd had an accident some other way. He wasn't new to ranching, but he wasn't an old, experienced hand, either. He'd only been out at Rancho Diablo for the better part of a year; he'd been here in this colossus all his life except for traveling the world doing business. This was a pretty secure environment. Insular, and protected by butlers and valets and a vigilant mother.

Anything could have happened at the ranch. It wouldn't do any good to feel guilty, at least not until Shaman telephoned Kendall with news.

Telling herself that didn't assuage the guilt.

Tempest rolled the pram from the austere white room and told herself there was time to work things out with Shaman. There had to be. They were still married—and hopefully, that was a starting point.

Even if her brother had done something terrible.

She felt sick, knowing that her marriage had probably been over before it had ever had a chance.

Chapter Eleven

Seeing Xav in the ICU scared Shaman. It was difficult looking at his younger brother with his eyes closed and tubes stuck in him. In his mind, Shaman always associated Xav with laughter and lightheartedness—happy-go-lucky, all-out life force. Kendall was the family stalwart, Gage the seeker, Shaman the wanderer.

"Open your eyes," he whispered to his brother. It was a plea. Xav lay so still and pale in the hospital bed, almost waxen, with the monitors assessing his vital signs.

Shaman hadn't mentioned to Sheriff Nance who he suspected might be behind the attacks on him and Xav. There was no real proof.

But he knew, deep in his gut. And though it had nearly destroyed his marriage, he knew he'd been right to make Tempest leave Dark Diablo.

Gage came in, eyeing Shaman with concern. "Are you all right?"

He nodded. "I'm fine."

"I'll be here for a while. Why don't you go take a break, get a cup of coffee."

"Thanks. I'll be back."

Gage settled into a chair. "No rush. I'm not leaving his side."

Shaman glanced at Gage. "You don't think it was an accident, either, do you?"

"No." He leaned back to get comfortable, crossing one boot over his leg. "The injury is too similar to yours. I think it's time we put a stop to it."

Shaman nodded. "I was thinking the same."

He left and drove to Tempest's small, run-down house, parking his truck and staring at the home where his wife had grown up. There was nothing here but bad memories—even Tempest had said that. She said the townspeople didn't tear it down because it was hers. Her fame kept it from being pushed over and splintered to bits, as Jonas had done to Bud Taylor's barns and bunkhouse.

It was best to clear out old ghosts.

Shaman went inside the small house, seeing a small propane cookstove on the floor. There was a battery-powered flashlight nearby and a hand-crank radio. On the dusty counter were two cartons of water bottles and a half-empty bottle of whiskey.

There was also a steel pipe leaning against the wall. Shaman examined it without touching it, not surprised to see blood streaks on the side.

If Bobby was in this house, Shaman knew he would kill him. Who would find out? Shaman knew how to do it quickly, quietly, without drama. He *wanted* to do it.

But he had two sons to think of. This was his wife's brother, even if there was no love lost between them. The best thing would be to let Bobby Taylor sit in jail for a long, long time.

Shaman pondered that. Then he called Sheriff Nance and reported a possible gas leak at his wife's old house. The sheriff didn't even question what Shaman was doing out there. A husband had every right to check on his wife's property for her.

That was what everyone would say.

Shaman left, making certain the flashlight was shining on the pipe like a beacon.

Then he went to church, something he hadn't done in years, and sat in a pew to pray, marshaling his thoughts. Then he lit a candle for Xav. He lit two for his sons and one for his wife, and finally, lit another one for what he was about to do.

TEMPEST HAD BEEN A LONER for so long that this new sense of familial guilt swamping her felt strange and overwhelming. Bobby must be thinking he could scare the Phillipses away from Dark Diablo. That would be his goal, because then all improvements on the property would cease. He was angry, lashing out at anyone who wanted to care for and grow Dark Diablo.

Painful as it was for her to acknowledge it, something had to be done about her brother. More importantly, she had to make changes in her own life. She couldn't go on expecting the Phillipses to clean up her problem. They'd already paid a heavy price.

Kendall rarely came down from her room, taking phone calls about Xav mostly in there. Millicent didn't demand the formal dinners she normally did, instead having her meals in her own suite. Tempest had been to her quarters a few times to check on Millicent and let her visit with her grandbabies, but even the twins couldn't cheer up their grandmother. She was too worried about Xav.

Tempest felt hollowed out by what she'd brought on this family that had taken her in and been so good to her.

She'd run from her past long enough.

She pushed the pram down the wide hall to find Kendall, knowing she'd be in the home office of Gil Phillips, Inc.

"Hi," Kendall said, glancing up from a giant oak desk where she sat staring at a computer screen. "I'm about to run to the hospital to see Xav."

"How is he?" Tempest asked. "Any change?"

"Unfortunately, no." She sighed. "I'm very afraid, actually."

"I know." Tempest was scared, too, and this was exactly why she'd come to say goodbye. "Kendall, I'm turning in my resignation."

Her eyes went wide. "No, you're not."

"I am. It's for the best. I find myself overwhelmed with the babies, and—"

"Bull-oney," Kendall said. "You're leaving because of what I told you, which is probably one of the very reasons Shaman didn't want you to know what had happened to him in the first place." She looked at Tempest with a determined expression. "And in fact, we don't actually know that your brother did it, remember."

"We know," Tempest said. "Shaman knows, or he wouldn't have tried to keep it from me."

His sister shrugged. "He's not going to be happy if you leave."

"I'll let him know where I am so he can see the boys whenever he wants to."

"So where will you be?"

"I'm going home," Tempest said.

"Not to the nasty place where Shaman said you grew up."

She flushed. "No."

"I'm sorry. I shouldn't have been so blunt. I didn't mean that quite the way it came out, Tempest. You know I admire you greatly, and everything you've accomplished. We wouldn't have hired you here if we didn't think highly of your talents."

"You hired me," Tempest said, "because you were trying to keep my children near you."

Kendall smiled. "Let me be clear, that's not exactly how Mom and I operate. If we'd just wanted to keep you here, we would have offered you anything for the sake of the children. But we don't hire any pity cases at Phillips, Inc. Only the best of the best—that's why we offered you a *job.* Mother and I actually felt a bit selfish for hiring you when you needed to be with your children. I told Mom you'd find work somewhere, either here or in London or New York or whatever. It turns out we are quite pleased with your performance."

Tempest smiled. "You're sweet. But not the world's most convincing actress." She rocked the pram with one foot, hearing the babies beginning to rustle around inside. "I'm going home to Tempest. I plan to live in the adobe bungalow that Shinny and Blanche rent to me, until I have time to think of what I want to build on my old property."

"Really," Kendall said. "Putting down roots at last?"

"I'm going to try."

"I still think you're leaving because of your half brother."

"I will admit to some feelings of guilt over what has happened," Tempest confessed.

Kendall nodded. "Just for the record, you can't control your half brother any more than I could control Gage, Shaman and Xav. Trust me, Mother and I have tried."

Tempest smiled. "Thank you for trying to make me feel better. I'm afraid it's quite impossible. Maybe when your brother is out of a coma and Bobby Taylor is in jail, then I'll feel better. For now, I just want to thank you for everything you and your mother have done."

"Whatever," Kendall said. "Just understand what this means. With you leaving I won't see my nephews as often. And Shaman likely won't pick up his duties in the family business. I suppose he'll park wherever you do." She gave a dramatic sigh that could have won an Oscar. "I am *not* happy."

Tempest smiled again. "When I build my house, I'll have guest rooms installed for visiting aunts and mothers-in-law."

"It's the least you can do," she replied. "I want my own en suite bath."

Tempest gazed at her warmly. "Goodbye, Kendall."

Kendall got up and kissed her nephews on their heads. "I do think you could have had one female, and named her after me."

Tempest pursed her lips. "No doubt you'll be next up to the altar, and can have your own legacy of little Millicent Kendalls."

Her sister-in-law shuddered. "I am not the maternal type."

"I didn't think I was, either. Always too busy." She smiled, realized it had once been true. "I had no idea how rewarding being a mother is. I wouldn't trade it for all the award shows and designer clothes in the world."

"Not me," Kendall declared. "I'm never trading my Manolo Blahniks for those Sperry loafers you wear all the time now."

Tempest grinned as she hugged her sister-in-law, knowing she was making the right decision for everyone. Then she put the babies in a car she borrowed from the Phillips fleet, and headed toward home.

SHERIFF JOHN NANCE WAS waiting for him when Shaman left the church.

"Saw your truck," the sheriff said. He leaned against an ivy-covered wall, looking like a big, tough hombre from south of the border, Clint Eastwood-style. "Thought I'd let you finish in there."

"What's up, Sheriff?" Shaman noted that the sun was beginning to drift a bit lower in the summer sky. He wondered what Tempest and his sons were doing, and felt good that they were safe in Hell's Colony. His anger rose a bit when he thought about Xav in the hospital, his head half opened by a thick lead pipe.

"Just thought you'd want to know we didn't find a gas leak at Tempest's house." The lawman leveled a probing gaze on him. "We did find evidence that someone's been living in the house. A vagrant or squatter, most likely."

Shaman waited, telling himself to be patient. Not much got past the sheriff.

"There was a door open, and the volunteer fire department boys and I went in to check for the possible leak. Why'd you leave?"

"My brother's in the hospital in ICU, Sheriff. There

was nothing left for me to do at my wife's old house, so I figured I'd let you do your job, and I'd get on to looking for some supernatural help for my brother."

Nance nodded. "We found the lead pipe you wanted us to find."

"Oh?" Shaman wasn't going to try to hoodwink the sheriff; he'd left clues that a child could figure out.

"Yeah. We're sending it for testing."

"I think you know who's been living in the house, Sheriff."

John Nance nodded. "I've heard rumors. I think you ought to know that we can't hold the man until we have evidence from the testing. It's always possible that the blood that's on that pipe isn't yours or your brother's. Why would Bobby Taylor leave it there?"

Shaman shrugged. "He didn't think he'd get caught. It's an effective weapon. He doesn't have to register for a gun. And he doesn't look so bright."

The lawman studied him. "Why you? Why your brother?"

"To get us away from Dark Diablo. Bobby Taylor believes that he got rooked out of his rightful inheritance, and he's determined to get it back, whether he has to sue someone or hurt them. I suspect he's run out of appeals and sympathetic ears for a lawsuit. It's expensive to pursue things through legal means. So his next plan is to get to Tempest. At least that's what I fear. He's taken over her old house. I'm certain it's occurred to him that if he can just run enough people off Dark Diablo, maybe he can take it over. Think about it, Sheriff," he said. "If…" Shaman's gaze was caught by a white Land Rover pulling into Shinny's Ice Cream Shoppe across the street. He was stunned when a tall, gorgeous blonde got out of it, and was thunderstruck as he watched her unpack a giant stroller with big rubber wheels. She placed his sons into it, then wheeled it into the ice cream shop.

His heart sank.

"Excuse me, Sheriff. I believe my wife just pulled into town, and I need to talk with her." As far as he was concerned, Tempest had better be here for a quick visit. Following that, he was going to send her right back to Hell's Colony.

Maybe she'd come to see him.

Instantly, he erased the hope. She would have called him if she'd wanted to see him. Shinny and Blanche were like parents to her; maybe she'd come to show them the babies. But Shaman wasn't going to allow her to stay long in town with a vengeful brother out for blood. Of course, this was the very problem that had gotten him in trouble with Tempest before: he didn't want her anywhere close to here until Bobby Taylor was in jail.

It was a sure thing she wouldn't be very happy if he had to tell her once again that he didn't think she should be in town.

Shaman pushed open the door and walked inside the cool, welcoming store. "Tempest," he said, and she turned to look at him. He missed her so much it hurt. He didn't think he'd ever get over the fact that this beautiful, independent woman was the mother of his children. It still stunned him that she'd allowed him to love her. He, the beast, had been fortunate beyond his wildest dreams.

"Yes, Shaman?"

He went to take one of his sons in his arms. "Why are you here? Why are my boys in Tempest?"

"We've come home," she said. "For good."

She didn't understand the danger. She didn't understand Bobby Taylor's determination.

"You can't stay," Shaman said, knowing that Sheriff Nance was behind him and listening to every word. "You can go to Rancho Diablo with the Callahans. Or you can go to Hell's Colony with my family. But Tempest cannot be your home right now. And I don't know when that will change."

There was a look of annoyance in her blue eyes as she retorted, "I believe we've had this conversation before, Shaman. This time, I'm doing what I believe is best. I know my brother hit you, and I'm sure he attacked your brother. I'm also sure you had your reasons for not telling me the truth about what happened. But to be frank, no one should be dealing with my brother Bobby except me. This is my town, this is my home, and we're not going anywhere."

Chapter Twelve

The conversation with Shaman hadn't gone well, but Tempest hadn't expected it to. He had his opinions, and he wanted to protect her. As much as she had allowed herself to fall in love with him—*allow* was a forgiving word, since she couldn't have stopped herself from falling in love with him if she'd wanted to—he was going to have to realize that this was her problem, not his.

It would be difficult to get that through an overprotective, ex-military soldier's head.

"Excuse me," she said, walking into the Tempest library. She smiled at the woman working behind the desk. "Is it possible to see the person who is in charge of the story time hour?"

"That would be me." The elderly woman with wire glasses and frizzy gray hair nodded at her. "I'm Ellen Dowdy. What can I do for you?"

Tempest pushed her hair back off her face. It was now or never; she was going to make herself get involved in the community, forge bonds with the place where her sons would grow up. They were going to have a different life than she'd had in Tempest. "My name is Zola Cupertino. I grew up here."

"I know." Ellen nodded. "I was your second-grade teacher."

Tempest smiled. "I remember you. I just didn't think you'd remember me."

"There's little in this town I don't know. What can I do for you?"

Tempest wondered at the woman's rather unwelcoming tone. "I've moved back here, permanently. I saw that you had story time sessions for the under three set, and I would like to volunteer my services."

Ellen sniffed. "The position is filled."

"Oh." Tempest was taken aback by Ms. Dowdy's abruptness. "Is there another time, perhaps, that needs volunteer readers?"

"I'm afraid not." She looked at her for a long moment. "Here's the thing. I remember when you were just a girl. Your mother wasn't much, and God knows your father was never around, but you were a sweet little thing. We were all proud of you when you went off to the big city and made something of yourself. But then you forgot about us. When you came home a few months back, you didn't come see any of us. You stayed in Blanche's bungalow and you drove around in your Land Rover, and as far as you were concerned, the rest of us didn't exist. I think you don't care about us or this town, and when you leave to go back to the bright lights, you'll never think of us again."

Tempest drew in a stunned breath. "Oh, Ms. Dowdy, I'm so sorry. It never occurred to me that my actions seemed like I didn't care about this town."

"Do you?" Ellen challenged. "Shinny and Blanche Tuck said they barely heard from you. After they practically raised you, too. If it hadn't been for them, you'd never have had anything."

Tempest blinked. Everything Ms. Dowdy said was true, in a way. She'd gotten busy with her career; she hadn't wanted to think much about the place where she'd been so unhappy. "You are right."

"I'm rarely wrong. So you think about that before you assume you're going to be the big star here." The librarian turned and went back to checking in books, dismissing her.

Tears welled in Tempest's eyes, but she blinked them back—fast. She left the library and went back to the ice cream shop.

"How'd it go?" Blanche asked when she walked in and sat in a booth. Blanche pushed the pram with the babies over to the table, and Tempest looked in at her tiny sons. They brought a smile to her face, which she needed.

"They don't have any openings," she said.

"Well, there's lots of ways to get involved here. You'll make friends, and you can— Are you crying?"

"No." Tempest shook her head and pulled a tissue from the boys' diaper bag. "I get allergies this time of year. Hay fever."

"Oh." Blanche glanced out the window. "You didn't run across Ms. Dowdy, did you?"

"We spoke briefly," she admitted. "Why?"

Blanche looked at her with some suspicion. "She can be a wee bit of a dragon at times. Depends on when you catch her. Could be a good mood or a really witchy mood. What mood was she in today?"

"I actually don't know her well enough to judge. She was my second-grade teacher. I'm still a bit in student mode with her, I'm sure." Tempest tried to smile, but she really felt low. So much of what Ms. Dowdy said was true. "Blanche, I'm so sorry if I didn't call often enough when I was gone."

Her friend snorted. "Long-distance phone calls used to cost an arm and a leg. Nowadays everyone's got a cell phone and it's not so bad, but back when you left, the only cheap rates were after eight o'clock on Sunday nights. Shinny and I never thought about it, to be honest. We didn't expect it." Blanche perked up. "Here comes your husband."

"Again?" Tempest turned to find Shaman strolling into the ice cream store. He was so big and handsome that it made her feel better just to look at him and realize all over again that he was her husband.

Then she wanted to smack him for being so pigheaded and outrageously stubborn.

"Hi," he said, leaning to kiss each of his babies.

"Hi," she replied, noting that he didn't give her a kiss, though he did buss Blanche noisily on her cheek. "I just saw you thirty minutes ago."

"Yeah. I know. I've been thinking about this problem of you living in Tempest, Cupertino." He scooted into the booth next to Blanche, which seemed to please her enormously.

Grinning, Blanche yelled, "Shinny, bring a few specials!"

Behind the counter, her husband nodded, waving at Shaman with a big smile.

"There is no problem with me living here," Tempest said, a trifle more irritably than she meant to.

"There is to me." Shaman drummed his fingers on the

table, considering her. She felt her blood pressure spike at his commanding tone, and unfortunately, also felt her heart turn a bit mushy at the fact that he was determined to be so devoted to her well-being.

"Where are you going to be staying?" he asked.

"In Shinny and Blanche's bungalow."

"Excellent." Shaman gave her a pleased smile that left no doubt in her mind as to his intentions. "So will I. We'll be one big happy family, you, me and the babies."

"I'm going to go check on those milkshakes," Blanche said, hopping up from the booth and leaving them to their discussion.

"Shaman, we're not going to live together," Tempest said.

"We're married. These are our children. They need to know that their parents are acting in their best interests. Us living under one roof is in their best interests." His smile was slow and easy, and Tempest's heart sped up like mad.

"All right," she said sweetly. "There's a sofa you can sleep on."

He smiled. "I hope you'll change your mind in due time about sleeping with me."

She wanted Shaman in her bed, but was too proud to admit it. And she still wasn't happy about him thinking he was going to take over her life, especially after he'd been dishonest with her. "I don't know, Shaman. You haven't been truthful about a lot of things with me."

He reached to take her hand in his, gently massaging her fingers. "I couldn't tell you about what your brother did. I never knew for certain if he was the one who attacked me. I still don't."

Tempest shook her head. "You could have at least mentioned that you thought it might have been him. I feel very responsible for Xav getting hurt."

"Why? I'm the one who should have thought Xav might be in danger. It never crossed my mind."

"None of this would have happened if…"

"If what, Cupertino? If Bud Taylor hadn't fallen in love with your mother? If he'd felt more love from his own children?" Shaman squeezed her fingers. "The only goal you and I have is to make sure these little babies know that their parents love them. Everything else is incidental."

She nodded. "You're probably right. I hope you are right. It's nice of you to try to make me feel better."

He kissed her fingers. "So…you'll invite me into your bed tonight?"

Smiling, she removed her hand from his. "Nice try, cowboy."

He grinned as Blanche put a famous Shinny special in front of him. "Thanks, darlin'."

Tempest wasn't certain she needed one of Shinny's high-calorie shakes, especially with all the baby weight she was still carrying. And most especially with the hunk across the table from her clearly stating his desire to get back in bed with her. Shaman winked.

Good thing the pram had huge rubber wheels on it, perfect for taking several laps around the town square. She needed all the exercise she could get, if her husband was going to keep that decidedly wolfish gleam in his eye.

"Well, look at you two." Bobby Taylor peered into the pram at the sleeping babies. "Apparently I have new nephews. The birth announcement must have gotten lost in the mail."

He slid into the booth next to his sister, grinning at her. Shaman stiffened, his face setting in hard, grim lines.

Bobby glanced at Tempest's milkshake. "If you're not going to drink that, I'll be happy to," he said, helping himself to the treat.

Tempest thought Shaman was going to reach across the table and throttle Bobby. His face was dark under his hat, his mouth flat, his eyes hard. Suddenly he looked like a soldier and not so much the man she'd fallen for.

"Taylor," Shaman said, "you have exactly two seconds to get out of this booth and leave the store before I throw you through the window."

Shinny hurried over, his round face sweating. "Can I help you with anything?"

"You might take the babies over to Blanche," Tempest said quickly. She was blocked from getting out of the booth by Bobby's big body.

Shinny promptly rolled the pram behind the counter. Bobby got up ever so slowly, his gaze on Shaman. "I know you were in my house today," he told him.

"It's not your house," Shaman said, his voice a growl.

"She doesn't want it," Bobby said. "Do you, sister? Lot of bad memories there for you."

"Tempest—"

"It's okay, Shaman." She glanced at Bobby, disgusted. "You're dancing on the thin edge of a knife, baiting him."

Bobby eyed Shaman. "He's not so much."

Tempest held up a hand to keep Shaman seated. "Just go, Bobby."

"He had the cops and fire department search your house today," her brother told her. "He came inside, nosed around, then called Sheriff Nance."

She looked at Shaman. "You went to my house today?"

Shaman nodded.

"Can I ask why?"

"I was hunting for him," Shaman said.

Tempest turned to Bobby. "Why did you attack my husband and my brother-in-law?"

Bobby looked at her. "I was protecting you."

Tempest blinked. "I don't need protection."

"You do. From him." Bobby glared at Shaman. "I don't think you realize what kind of people they are. Your husband was a military operative—"

"That has nothing to do with me," Tempest said. "He's not going to hurt me."

"You need to think twice about being married to him. You can't trust him." Bobby sent a sly glance Shaman's way. "Once a killer, always a killer."

She gasped. "That's a terrible thing to say!"

"It's terrible that he's the father of those two precious little babies," Bobby said woefully. "Anyway, I had to do it. They had no business being in my father's house."

"Shaman and Xav are employed by Jonas Callahan, who owns the property," Tempest stated, barely hanging on to her temper.

"I'm going," Shaman said. "Because if I don't, he's going to be eating a plate glass window."

"Nah, don't go." Bobby finished off the milkshake. "I just came to see my nephews and my dear sister. I've had my say."

"Bobby," Tempest said quietly. "I am not your sister.

You are not my brother. My brother wouldn't have tried to kill my husband, nor my brother-in-law. Those are not your nephews. If I ever catch you near my children, you and I will find ourselves at cross-purposes."

"Zola, listen," Bobby said. "I know our father left you his estate. I know you gave my inheritance away. You didn't have to do that—you could have split it with all of us. You don't think there'll be a reckoning eventually?"

Her skin chilled. Thank goodness Shaman remained still, his muscles and jaw tight, his body crouched—but unmoving. Not entirely murderous. "Go. I don't ever want to see you again."

Bobby got up, smirking, and left, jutting his chin at Shaman as he ambled to the door.

Tempest realized she was shaking. With fear and with rage.

"You all right?" Shaman asked.

"I'm fine." She thought she was going to be ill.

"You see why you couldn't stay at Dark Diablo. He's crazy." Shaman came around and scooted into the booth beside her.

"You went into my house today. You were looking for him. You were going to hurt him," Tempest said.

"Hurt him?" Shaman frowned at her. "I was simply checking up on him."

She shook her head. "You cannot kill him, Shaman."

He didn't say anything.

"This isn't your fight. It's mine. You've just gotten caught up in it," she said, feeling desperate.

"I like a good fight. Haven't run from one yet." He put his hand over hers. "Don't worry about me."

She was. She was worried about her husband, her

brother-in-law and her children. The danger had come here because of her.

"Shaman, I don't need a bodyguard. Or a hired gun. Whatever you think you are." She fixed him with a mutinous glare. "I also don't appreciate you stalking my half brother. He's an oily snake, but I can handle this."

The words rose to her lips, words she didn't want to speak, but which had to be said if all the bad things were finally going to come to an end. "Shaman, we agreed to be married until after the babies were born." She took a deep breath. "I think it's best if we call an end to this pretend marriage."

Chapter Thirteen

Shaman's heart seemed to shatter. He stared at his wife, wondering why she didn't love him as much as he loved her. They had children together.

Divorce?

He hoped she was just upset because of Bobby.

"Cupertino, you're the only woman I've ever wanted," he said quietly. "Give us some time."

"All we've had is time." She looked at him, her eyes sad. "We're too far apart, too different, Shaman."

Blanche wheeled over the pram. "I think these handsome fellows are getting hungry. They're too young to eat a Shinny special just yet." She smiled at them, but her eyes flicked nervously to Shaman. "Everybody all right?"

"We're fine. Thanks, Blanche," he answered.

Shaman took a baby out of the stroller and handed him to Tempest. He picked up the other one and took the bottle Blanche held out. "Thanks."

"What are you doing?" Tempest asked, her blue eyes wide as he propped the baby in the angle of his arm.

"Feeding my son. Which one do I have, anyway?"

She sighed. "Gage."

"Figures. I always did have to look out for my older

brother." He glanced over at the baby she was feeding. "Do you call him Shaman or Jonas?"

"I combined the two names and call him Josh. It would be too confusing to call both of you Shaman, and same goes for Jonas, since we run into him so much. So it's Gage and Josh."

"I like it," Shaman said, running the names through his mind. "After I get little man here calmed down, I'm going to call and check on Xav. Then I think you and I should finish our discussion."

"There's nothing to discuss."

There was plenty to discuss. If she thought she was going to kick him to the curb just because she was scared, he needed to do some convincing that everything was going to be fine.

If she didn't love him and couldn't ever see herself loving him, well, that would be a whole other spiny cactus to walk into. But he had to find out. "Cupertino, I know you don't know this because I haven't told you, but I'm really happy about these little bundles of joy."

"I am, too." She gazed down fondly at the baby in her arms, and Shaman thought he'd never seen a more beautiful woman. "I remember when I started thinking about having a baby. You were hinting around about wanting one—"

He laughed. "Not me, doll. That idea was all yours. And Cat's. I was just happy to be invited to try out for the part of devoted dad."

"And then you mentioned you wanted to marry me first," Tempest said, glaring at him for interrupting her story. "I just have this funny feeling that if we'd done everything the traditional way—"

"It was very traditional, Cupertino. You haven't given me a chance to really romance you."

She looked at him, her lips parted for just a moment, then shook her head. "I mean, that if we'd gotten married first and then tried to get pregnant, I don't know that I'd be any happier. We might not even have these little guys. And to be honest, I'm happier now than I ever was in my career. When I was in show biz, I wanted to be a hermit when I wasn't on stage. Now I want to stroll around town with the babies, meet people, talk to folks I haven't seen in years."

She let Josh circle her finger with his tiny fist as he fed, and a smile dawned on her face. Shaman's heart contracted. He could almost see the bond developing between mother and son, and it was more amazing than anything he could ever have imagined.

If I'd known I'd have this in my life when I got out of the military, I would have been a whole hell of a lot more sane when I was over there.

"I even applied for story time at the library today."

"You have to apply for story time?" Shaman asked.

"Of course." She sighed. "They turned me down, but I'll find some other way to start reintroducing myself to Tempest."

"How can they turn you down? You donated a ton of money to the library."

"Several hundred thousand dollars." She shrugged. "Ms. Dowdy doesn't know that. Only the lawyer knows, remember?"

Shaman frowned. "They just didn't have any openings?"

"Oh, I think they probably always have openings. Ms.

Dowdy felt I've gotten a bit too big for Tempest. Do you mind moving out of the booth? I need to walk Josh after I feed him. It's the only way I can get a burp out of him. Gage belches like a smokestack, but this one requires a little walk and rock."

Shaman moved out of her way. "Cupertino," he said, as she slid out, "don't divorce me yet. I don't know these babies, and I don't really know you."

"I don't know you, either," she said, her voice soft. "But I don't want you trying to hurt Bobby. He may be horrible, but he's not going to harm me."

Shaman bit the inside of his cheek, wanting to rebut her words. How could he be certain? Of course Bobby might want to hurt her—he was convinced she'd given away his birthright. He'd said so. "I don't know that I can promise you that."

"I know you can't." She gazed at him sadly. "And I understand how you feel. Until Xav makes it, you have every right to be mad. Furious. Angry." She took a deep breath. "Even more because he also attacked you. I understand that. But I want to let Sheriff Nance handle it. And I don't think your pride and your instincts for vengeance will allow that."

She was asking a lot of him. Shaman swallowed hard. "I'll agree if you let me stay in the bungalow with you and the boys."

Her eyes went wide. Josh burped, and she rubbed his little back, then gently replaced him in the pram, straightening his tiny blue T-shirt and navy blue bottoms. She took Gage from him, smiling with satisfaction when Gage blew a burp that would have made the Callahan brothers proud—Shaman was pretty impressed himself—and put him next to his brother, tucking them together for their nap. Then she looked up at him.

"All right," she said. "Just until Sheriff Nance has this all sorted out. If you don't try to exact any revenge on Bobby yourself. It shouldn't take long for the sheriff to pull all the pieces together. I'll ask Shinny if he has an extra key."

She walked off, pushing the pram, and Shaman didn't even think to ask her where she was going, or even to say goodbye. He was so thunderstruck that she'd actually said he could stay with her that he sank back in the booth, relieved.

He could spend a lot of time with his sons.

He could do a little casual, inauspicious wooing of his wife. At least she hadn't mentioned the *D* word again, because he certainly didn't want a divorce.

He wanted a marriage.

The only problem was, he'd made a promise he wasn't certain he could keep. He wasn't as trusting as his sweet wife, and as far as Shaman was concerned, something had to be done about Taylor. He was itching to pull Bobby's head from his shoulders and...

Shaman took a deep breath. He'd made a promise.

And if the promise he'd made was the only way he was going to get into his wife's house, then he'd just have to eat a little crow and behave where Taylor was concerned.

But if Bobby got anywhere near Tempest or his sons with the same intention as what he'd pulled on him and Xav, then all bets were off.

It was not going to be easy to turn off the protective soldier that still lurked inside him.

"THIS IS HOME SWEET HOME," Tempest said, opening her front door. She pushed the pram inside and Shaman followed her silently, picking up a baby once they were there. She got the other twin out, and turned to the man who was her husband, though she still couldn't believe that.

He wouldn't be for much longer.

"This is the sofa where you can sleep. It's a pullout," Tempest said. "Shinny designed this place to sleep a family of six. There are two and a half baths, so you'll have your own. Really, there's no reason we have to come in contact with each other that often."

He nodded, holding Josh to him, cradling the baby's head.

She wouldn't admit it to Shaman, but she felt better with him here. Perhaps that didn't make sense. She knew they'd divorce sooner rather than later, but she also remembered how kind and loving he was. He'd changed her life, even if he hadn't meant to. And it was all for the better.

She was a little afraid of Bobby, though she wouldn't admit it. Nothing would happen to her or the children with Shaman here.

"I have an ulterior motive in letting you stay here," she said. "Beyond the basic caring of the children."

"Diaper duty isn't why you're giving me the sofa?" he asked, raising a brow.

"Partially," she said, her tone cool. "I want to keep an eye on you. I don't trust you not to make Bobby's life miserable."

"You're still not being honest," Shaman said.

"What does that mean?" Tempest demanded, suspecting she knew very well. He was referring to when she'd first met him, and began visiting him. She felt a blush rise on her cheeks.

He was right. She wasn't being honest.

"We belong together, Cupertino." He sank onto the sofa with his son. "Never mind that right now. Hand me the other tyke."

"You can't hold two."

Shaman laughed. "When I was six, I carried Kendall and Xav across a street because they were too afraid to cross it. I know twins, doll. Give me my brother's namesake."

Reluctantly, she handed him Gage. The baby settled into his arm, and he held Josh across his lap. Both babies were too satisfied from their feedings to do more than snooze with contentment. They barely noticed they'd been moved.

"You go shower or whatever you need to do," Shaman said.

"I do need to store some breast milk."

He held up a hand. "Consider me on diaper duty."

She thought he'd looked a bit squeamish about the mention of breast milk. "Call me if you need anything."

"We won't. The three of us are going to catnap."

He did look tired. Tempest went into her bedroom, relaxing a bit now that Shaman was with them. No one would dare mess with him. Shaman looked wild-eyed as it was, and he was tall and big and sturdy. Handsome.

She was madly in love with him.

It was not good to be in love with a man you knew you couldn't stay with.

She was lost in her thoughts and wondering where the

happy ending was when she realized her makeup had been scattered across the marble counter in the bathroom. Tempest gasped, and fear skittered through her as she read the words that had been scrawled on her bathroom mirror.

I'm watching you.

Her heart thundered, her knees weakened. He'd been here—in the only place in the world besides her villa in Tuscany that felt like home. This B and B was her special place, the home she ran to when she needed comfort.

Shaman was right: Bobby wasn't going to stop.

She peeked around the corner at Shaman. He was sleeping comfortably with his sons, her three guys snug and happy to be together. Shaman had had a long, stressful day, too, with Xav's accident.

Which of course had been no accident.

There was only one thing to do.

She slipped out the door past Shaman into the twilight. She was the one Bobby Taylor hated for giving away what he thought was his. She'd been protecting him, understanding what it was like not to feel you had a base, a touchstone.

She drove to her house, the tiny shack where she'd grown up and where she knew she'd find her half brother. She walked inside the house, not hearing anything. "Hello? Bobby?"

No answer. She waited another moment, her heart hammering, the blood rushing painfully in her ears. If she didn't do this, Shaman would do something rash and find himself in deep trouble. She knew too well that he wasn't geared for patience.

There was nothing else to do. Only good things rose

up from cleared ground; the future could have a happy ending only if the past was burned away.

She took a deep breath and looked at the caved-in sofa where her mother used to sit and wait for Bud Taylor to call.

Tempest needed to be free of the past, once and for all.

She saw a pack of cigarettes across the room on the kitchen counter. Bobby smoked. A shiver ran over her at this evidence of her half brother living in her house. She moved to the counter and picked up a book of matches, turning it over with her fingers.

No. As much as she wanted to destroy this place and flush Bobby out, she couldn't do it. There had to be another way to cut the ties with the past.

She walked out the front door and drove away.

BANGING ON THE FRONT DOOR woke Shaman from the soundest sleep he'd had in days. He'd been dreaming that he was in bed with Tempest, and she was naked and willing, like she'd been when she'd first come to the farmhouse.

He did not want to lose that dream.

He settled the babies carefully on the sofa, putting pillows around them so they wouldn't roll off. "Who is it?"

"Sheriff Nance."

Shaman opened the door. "Howdy, Sheriff. Come on in. I'm watching the little men."

Sheriff Nance eyed the sleeping babies. "Wish I felt that peaceful."

"Everybody does. Tempest is in the back, if you're wanting to talk to her."

"I don't think she's here," the sheriff said.

Shaman shoved a hand through his hair, commanding himself to wake up faster. "Yeah, she is. She said something about needing to put away some breast milk. Tempest!" he called. "Will you watch the boys for a second, Sheriff? I'll get her."

He walked into the back of the bungalow, peering around rooms he'd never seen before. "Tempest?" The rooms smelled like her—wonderful—and he wondered how he could bear it if she told him she really wanted their marriage to be over. "Tempest?"

He walked into the bathroom, his stomach tightening like a fist when he saw the words scrawled across the bathroom mirror. "Dear God," he muttered.

He strode back out to the den. "You're right. She's not here."

"Kinda figured." The sheriff had settled himself next to the babies, and now he didn't look up. He kept his gaze on the boys for a long moment. "The old Cupertino place burned to the ground about a half hour ago."

Shaman's blood froze. He looked at the sheriff, who met his gaze without blinking. "I see."

The sheriff nodded. "I need to search this place."

"Don't you need a warrant?" Shaman asked.

The lawman handed him one.

"Damn. I was hoping you'd need to go get it."

Sheriff Nance shook his head. "Things move pretty fast around here when necessary." He walked past Shaman, who heard him stepping through the rooms. This could only mean one thing: the sheriff thought Tempest had burned down her home. The only reason she might do that was to flush Bobby out. Knowing that her half brother had been in the B and B and had threatened her would make Tempest furious—and frightened for her children. She was far too independent to let anybody push her around, and the tiger instinct had probably risen to the fore because of the boys. Shaman glanced at his sons, not surprised when Sheriff Nance came down the hall, his face wreathed with annoyance.

"You weren't going to mention the love letter on the mirror back there?" he asked.

"I just saw it myself. Trust me, Sheriff, I'm in the dark here."

Nance nodded. "Shaman, I'm going to have to take her in for questioning on suspicion of arson."

Shaman glanced at his sons. They were both sleeping soundly, blissfully unaware that their peaceful lives were about to be changed forever. "You don't know that Tempest did it."

"People saw her Land Rover driving out that way."

Shaman shook his head. "Means nothing. You know very well that Bobby Taylor's been squatting there. He could have dropped a match."

"He could have, but I just saw him at Cactus Max's."

"The house was old, ramshackle. It was a firetrap waiting to happen."

Sheriff Nance nodded. "I like that theory the best of all. I love Tempest just like you do, just like this town does. She put us on the map." He took a deep breath. "The problem is that Bobby's bringing charges. He says she tried to kill him, since Tempest's car was seen in the area, going down the lane to her old home. The law's the law and has to treat everyone fairly, even roaches like Bobby."

"And the love letter on the mirror? Come on, Sheriff. You know he was threatening his sister."

"That I don't know. I don't even know that you didn't write that note."

"I don't write with lipstick when I have a point to make. And I don't do much threatening. I'm a man of few words, and spring-loaded for action." Bobby had finally found a way to spring a trap on his half sister. "I'm afraid you're mistaken. That Land Rover you saw isn't Tempest's."

The sheriff studied him. "Oh?"

"Check the registration papers inside. You'll see it's owned by Gil Phillips, Inc., or what we like to call The Family, Inc." He smiled grimly, glancing one last time at his sons. "That's my car you saw going down the lane. And I started the fire. You know I was in the church, where I went to ask God Almighty to forgive me for what I was about to do."

That part was absolutely true; Tempest had just beaten him to the punch. "Bobby Taylor laid open my skull and then my brother's, and to be honest, it's in my DNA to take a man out when necessary. Burning down Tempest's house means Bobby Taylor has no place left to go in this town."

Nance stared him down, then shook his head. "All right, soldier. Call Shinny and Blanche to watch these bed fleas of yours, so I can take you in."

"Thanks, Sheriff."

The lawman let out a long breath. "Don't thank me. I don't know how long I'm going to buy your story."

"At least until I can get Tempest to go to my family's home in Hell's Colony," Shaman said.

"I'll give you until tomorrow," the sheriff said. "And good luck with that. Zola Cupertino always made her own decisions."

Shaman knew that. He loved that about her. But this was the way it had to be.

Chapter Fourteen

"Uncle Shaman," Cat said ruefully, looking through the bars of the Tempest jail. "What are you doing in prison? Dad says you're the rebel in the family. All brains, all glory. Is that why you're here?"

Shaman grimaced and stuck a hand through the bar to ruffle Cat's hair. "I'm not really in jail. I'm…thinking deep thoughts. This is where I do it. It's quiet."

"Yeah, right." Cat grinned. "Dad said a bad word when Kendall called to say you needed to be sprung. She helicoptered in a couple lawyers so you'd be represented properly. It's pretty wild in the courthouse right now. Dad says that'll teach you not to be tossing Molotov cocktails and pulling military stunts in small towns, which is what he figured you did, because you never do anything halfway."

"That's so nice," Shaman said. "I appreciate my brother's support."

"Aunt Kendall said she'd be here, too, except that Uncle Xav woke up and she's not leaving his side. He's going to be fine." Cat's pixie face perked up with delight. "He said to tell you he wished he was here with you to raise hell, and that really made Aunt Kendall mad. She says there's something in the H_2O in Tempest that's made all her brothers certifiable."

He tried to peer out the window toward the courthouse as Cat rambled through her laundry list of family gossip. "Do you know where Cupertino is? Where my sons are?"

"I heard her down the hall trying to sweet-talk Deputy Keene into letting her have the key to your cell."

Shaman turned back to Cat. "The key? Why?"

She shrugged. "I don't know. She told me to go take a look at my numskull uncle." Cat smiled at him. "I think that means she's not happy with you."

"I've been in the doghouse with her a long time." Shaman wished it wasn't true, but he didn't think anything was likely to change very soon.

Tempest appeared next to Cat, looking like a sweet dream. She wore blue jeans and loafers and a T-shirt that read I Love NY. Her hair was in a knot on her head, she had on no makeup, and she was the sexiest lady he'd ever seen.

"Hi," she said, unlocking the cell. She stared at him a long moment before seating herself on the wooden bench beside him. "Idiot. What were you thinking?"

"Hello to you too, gorgeous. Boy, are you a sight for sore eyes."

Cat seated herself next to Tempest.

"Oh, honey, I don't know if your daddy wants you in a jail cell," Tempest said.

"I know," Cat said. "He's probably going to say that Shaman's dragging the family down. He said he always did have to dig Uncle Shaman out of trouble."

"That is not how the story goes, niece. I'll straighten

your father's faulty memory out later. Where are my sons?" he asked Tempest.

"With Shinny and Blanche. They said this is not a healthy environment for them." She looked at Shaman. "Why did you tell Sheriff Nance that you did it?"

"Because I was going to," he admitted. "It's just coincidence that the house went up before I could."

"This is so dumb," Tempest said. "You're sitting in jail and Bobby the rat is free."

"I'm thinking I'm going to build you a new house for a wedding present," Shaman said. "That adobe bungalow you live in is too small for my sons. I figure they're going to be big boys. They'll need a basketball court and a soccer field and some horses. An upstairs for their own hangout, and cabinets for their rodeo buckles."

Tempest sighed. "Let's not talk about anything except how we're going to get you out of this."

"It's going to be all right, Aunt Tempest," Cat said. "Aunt Kendall said she'd sent in the Marines to get Uncle Shaman out of the mess he made. She said these lawyers are the best in the business."

Tempest giggled. "You do not fully appreciate your sister's strength."

"Yeah. I do. Believe me, Kendall is stronger than all of us." Shaman sighed, about to protest about the two of them sitting in the cell with him when Fiona Callahan appeared. She was dressed in pink from head to toe, complete with a straw hat decorated with pink flowers. Just looking at her made Shaman grin. "Howdy, stranger."

"If ever cookies were needed, I'd say now is the time." Fiona looked at Cat with some concern. "Honey, does your daddy know where you are?"

"Yes," she said with a grave shake of her head. "I'm supposed to check on him while Dad's at the courthouse."

Fiona looked at Shaman. "Jonas brought Sam because he said you needed a crack lawyer. Kendall sent her team, and Gage said the place was crawling with so many lawyers it put his teeth on edge. He said you were so lawyered up no one would ever suspect you were just a poor cowboy. I hitched a ride so I could bring you and Tempest a baby gift." She seated herself on the long bench, and smiled as Cat took a pink-sprinkled cookie.

"Good thing I'm a model child," Cat said.

Fiona laughed. "True." She handed a small blue-polka-dotted bag to Tempest. "These are for the babies."

She smiled back. "Thank you so much."

Fiona looked at Shaman. "You'll recognize this, I feel certain."

Tempest pulled two pairs of tiny knitted sky-blue baby booties from the bag, and then two knitted baby blankets in beautiful blue-and-white mixed yarns. "Fiona, they're lovely! Did you knit these yourself?"

"I did." She smiled with delight at Shaman. "I did a much better job after your husband showed me where I was going wrong with my knitting."

Tempest looked at him. "Knitting?"

He shrugged. "It's peaceful. Isn't it, Fiona?"

She laughed. "When I'm not dropping stitches."

He took a baby blanket from Tempest, examining it carefully. "Thank you, Fiona. The boys are going to love your gifts."

Shaman looked up as an elderly, square-set woman walked into the cell. "Welcome," he said. "Join the knitting club."

"I'm Ellen Dowdy," she replied. "Quite a ruckus you're causing out there," she told Shaman.

"Ms. Dowdy," Tempest said, "I'd like to introduce you to my husband, Shaman, my niece, Cat Phillips, and Fiona Callahan of Rancho Diablo in Diablo."

Ellen nodded. "Good to meet everyone. Heard your house burned, Zola. I should say I'm real sorry to hear it, but I'm not. Unlike other folks in this town who wanted to make a shrine of it, I thought it was a roach motel that should have been knocked over years ago. I hope you're not sad about it."

"No, ma'am, I can't say that I am," she said, and Shaman took her hand in his.

"Well, I hope you'll be staying in Tempest, anyway." Ellen looked at the knitted booties and blankets in Tempest's lap. "We have knitting and sewing circles here, and we have a position open at the library for a storyteller if you're still of a mind to read to our kids." She squared her jaw at everyone in the room. "There's also need for a drama teacher at the elementary school, which I am certain you have the appropriate résumé and experience to handle."

"Really?" Tempest said. "I would love that!"

Ellen nodded. "I hope you'll plan on staying here. Goodbye," she said politely to the cell at large, then disappeared, her soft-soled shoes making no noise on the concrete floor.

"Wow, Aunt Tempest," Cat said. "You're going to be famous in Tempest."

She smiled. "I wonder what made her change her mind?"

"Oh, folks with that much age and spice in them generally come to the right decision in due time," Fiona said, and Shaman chuckled.

"Congratulations." He squeezed Tempest's fingers.

"You guys can't stay in here forever," Deputy Keene said. "Sheriff Nance'll be annoyed that this place is becoming a regular meet-n-greet." He glanced at the plate of cookies in Fiona's lap, which she offered to him. After a moment, he snatched two, muttering, "Ten more minutes can't hurt anything," and trundled back down the hall.

"I suppose I should go," Fiona said. "Cat, let's you and I go see if Uncle Sam has managed to spring Shaman from his misdeeds." She shook her head at him. "One would think a house that decrepit would have fallen down with a good puff of wind. Sorry, Tempest, no insult to your home."

"None taken," she said quickly. "Goodbye, Fiona. Thank you for the cookies and the lovely gifts."

Fiona flopped a hand at them and disappeared. Cat followed after flinging her arms around both of them for a hug, then hurried to follow her nana.

Tempest leaned her head against Shaman's shoulder and sighed. "Why are you protecting me?"

He closed his eyes, enjoying the feel of her against him. It felt like home. Everything about Tempest felt like the home he'd always been searching for. "I always will," he said. "I promised to love, honor and protect you, and you promised to love, honor and obey me. I believe you emphasized obedience."

"Nice try, but I don't think so."

"Okay," Shaman said, smiling. "I can compromise on

the obeying part. But I'm always going to protect you, and my children."

"You may be in jail a long time," Tempest said. "I guess the boys and I can bring you meals on occasion."

"I ate MREs for years. I can handle Sheriff Nance's grub."

She looked at him. "I'm going to tell Sheriff Nance the truth, Shaman. I'm going to tell him you didn't do it."

"He won't believe you," Shaman said. "You just take care of my sons."

"But you didn't do it."

"That's true," Shaman said, "but I can't have the mother of my children in jail. I'd say it'd be pretty hard to feed those hungry boys of mine if you're in here."

She sat up, staring at him. "Wait a minute. Are you saying you think I set the fire?"

He looked at her. "The sheriff seemed to think so. You'd left the bungalow, so—"

She shook her head. "Shaman, I went to the house. I walked down memory lane. But I didn't burn it down."

He considered that. "Bobby told the sheriff he saw your car at the house. He said you went inside."

"Because I did. But I promise I didn't commit arson."

Shaman studied her for a long moment, seeing truth in her blue eyes. Then it hit him. "Holy crap, Tempest. You've been set up. Bobby wants you to go to jail because he wants to see you suffer."

"Yeah. He had a great plan. But you took the fall." She shook her head at him. "You're my hero, but you're going to have to figure out that I really can take care of myself."

She put her hand in his and Shaman felt hope flare to life inside him. "I know you can. Believe me, I know it." He let out a long, deep breath. "Bobby's got us in a heckuva bind. I confessed, and if I rescind my confession, you're going to jail because we can't prove that Bobby did it. And he did, or he wouldn't have covered his tracks by telling the sheriff he saw you out there."

"He was in the house when I was there," Tempest said, with sudden realization. "I noticed a pack of cigarettes on the counter."

Shaman remembered getting broadsided with the pipe, remembered what Xav looked like in ICU. Tight, fierce anger washed over him as he thought of what could have happened to Tempest if Bobby had decided to take his fury out on her.

"You just stay close to me until this is over," he said. "I'm gonna crush Bobby like a bug if I ever see him."

"I'll help you."

She didn't say anything else, but she snuggled a little closer to him. And it filled his heart with hope.

"ALL RIGHT, HERO. You're free to go." Sheriff Nance opened the cell, shaking his head at Shaman. "You know you didn't save anybody."

Shaman looked around for Tempest. He'd fallen asleep because it had felt so darn good to have her lying against his shoulder. At some point she'd left, which was pretty typical of their relationship.

She was going to have to stop leaving and start staying.

"I'm not trying to be a hero. Why are you letting me miss the Thursday night edition of 'Jailhouse Rock'?"

"Very funny, soldier. Go before I change my mind." He shut the cell behind Shaman. "By the way, I didn't make a report that you confessed. I know you were lying. The question is why. I'd really appreciate you breaking the unfortunate habit of lying to people in uniform."

"You were the first." Shaman didn't move down the hall the way he knew the sheriff wanted him to. "Where is my wife?"

"She's not here. I think she went to feed the babies. She can't babysit you all the time." Nance grinned at his joke. "If I were you, I'd get over to the courthouse. Your people have made a stink the like of which we've never seen in this town, and I suspect we'll be talking about it for years. We don't usually get this much excitement, although with you and Zola around, things are looking up."

"I don't have 'people.'"

"You have an army of lawyers and about four or five family members. If everyone leaves, I'll be able to get on with my job."

Shaman stayed right where he was, not about to take a step down the hall until he knew that Tempest wasn't going to be hauled in to jail. "If you're letting me go, who do you think burned down Tempest's house?"

"I have my suspicions," Sheriff Nance said, "but right now we're just going to call it a plain old unfortunate accident in a house that should have been razed long ago. These things happen in abandoned places. Old wiring gets chewed through by mice, and so forth."

Shaman nodded. "Pesky little buggers."

"Exactly. So go before I lock you up again just for annoying me. Or loitering. That's always good for about twenty-four hours in the slammer."

Shaman hesitated. "So Tempest and I are in the clear?"

Sheriff Nance shrugged. "As long as you don't go

making any more heroic confessions to save your wife, you're probably fine."

"Thanks." He headed down the hall and out into the late-afternoon sun. The town square looked as if a festival of some kind was being celebrated there. He doubted there'd ever been this much traffic in Tempest.

There was no time to see what all the excitement was about over there; someone would tell him soon enough. He headed over to Shinny's Ice Cream Shoppe to find Tempest.

"Hi, Blanche," he said as he walked through the door.

"Well, if it isn't the town hero." She gave him a broad smile. "That sure was good of you to rescue Bobby Taylor from that burning house. I know you two have no love lost between you."

"I didn't rescue Bobby from anything. In fact, I might have tossed him in if I'd had the chance. Let him take a personal tour of Dante's *Inferno*." Shaman glanced around. "Do you know where Tempest is?"

"She took the babies back to the bungalow so they could eat and nap." Blanche grinned. "Those sure are sweet little boys. Reminds me of their mother when she was a wee thing. You never saw such an ugly baby in your life, though." She laughed at the memory. "Red and wizened and always yelling. She had colic, you know. And no hair."

Shaman blinked. "My wife is drop-dead gorgeous. She makes men run into light posts. Why are you telling me my fabulous, sexy wife was an ugly kid?"

"Ah, well. That was then and this is now." Blanche wiped down a counter, then paused thoughtfully. "You know, it's a funny thing, but she and Bobby Taylor never looked a bit alike. Guess that's because they had different mothers."

Shaman turned, his hand on the doorknob. "They don't look alike now. He's a blockhead of stupidity and she's an angel. He's dumber than a rock and it shows on his greedy face. My lady would give you the hat off her head if you needed it to stay out of the rain."

Blanche smiled. "All true."

He looked at her. "Who was Bobby Taylor's mother?"

"Clara Jane Simmons."

"What happened to her?" He had a funny feeling he was missing some information, and Blanche was trying to help him see the light.

"She died. She was a nice lady. But she missed her people and she'd had those three boys and I don't think she cared for living out at what is now Dark Diablo. It was lonely and Bud Taylor was gone a lot. She got some infection and died." Blanche shrugged. "I went to her funeral. Bud Taylor was a mess, I can tell you. I don't know that he loved his wife, but he sure didn't want to be left alone with three young boys."

"Young?"

"Pretty much. I'd say Bobby was probably eight at the time, his siblings younger."

Shaman let go of the doorknob and went back over to the counter. "How many years until he took up with Tempest's mother?"

"Right after. Men don't tend to wait long. They don't live without a woman too well. Anyway, it was just a casual thing for a while, and then Zola was born." Blanche washed out some ice cream glasses and dried them with a paper towel. "She started school, of course, six years later. Bobby was about fourteen then. The kids gave him hell about his sister, because everybody knew. We didn't know for sure, but we suspected."

"Poor Cupertino," Shaman said.

"Yeah. I don't think it was easy for her. Anyway, Bobby's been festering about being the butt of those jokes for years. Then the old man died and didn't leave any of them a dime. And they never knew what happened to the money."

Shaman knew. "Why would Bobby Taylor take all this out on Tempest?"

"I suspect as a child he was afraid that his father might fall in love with her mother. And then Zola was born, an instant rival. She went off and got famous, he stayed here and made a mess of his life. You wonder why you don't see his siblings around these parts?" She put the glasses in the cupboard. "Because they made something of themselves. And they didn't care to live in the past like Bobby did. But I still say Tempest was such a neglected, hungry kid that none of this matters."

"You think Mr. Taylor would have helped out with some money when she was young, if she was his. If he believed she was his."

"Would be a likely thing to happen."

Maybe Bud Taylor had felt guilty that he'd never helped his only daughter out when she was young, and thus he'd left her all his money.

"Hi," Tempest said, pushing the pram through the door. "I went to see you at the jail, but Sheriff Nance said he'd let you go. Said you were getting on his last nerve." She smiled. "Sheriff Nance's nerves are not the thing to get on the wrong side of, just in case you weren't aware, Shaman."

He looked at his darling and opinionated wife. He thought about blockhead Bobby and his wide face. None of Blanche's hints made sense. If Tempest wasn't Bud Taylor's daughter, then why did everyone think she was?

Gage let out a squawk, and his brother added to the noise. "You sure are loud little men," Shaman said, picking his children up from the pram, holding one in each arm. "Loud, but good lookers, too. It's clear you get your looks from your mother."

Blanche and Tempest laughed. "They are Phillipses," Tempest said. "I was not a beautiful baby. Somewhere Blanche has some baby pictures of me, and you can see that for yourself."

He blinked. "You couldn't have ever been ugly, Tempest."

She smiled. "Haven't you ever heard of the ugly duckling, Shaman? The fortunate thing for our boys is that they have good genes from your side of the family tree."

"Yeah," Shaman said, gazing down at his sons. "Not so much mine, though. That was Xav's arena. I was the thinker, and Gage was the wild one."

"No," Tempest said, "your sister says you and Gage tied for the wild prize. You always tried to do him one better. She said you felt a need to prove yourself."

Most men did. Shaman kissed his babies on their soft, fuzzy heads, thinking. "When was the last time you saw your mother's husband, Cupertino?"

"I don't know." Tempest frowned at him. "Mac Cupertino came by to visit a time or two, maybe three or four, throughout my childhood. I was probably twelve the last time I saw him." Her face had darkened. "He died about five years ago. Why do you ask?"

Blanche smiled, and came to take little Gage from Shaman's arms. Shinny walked into the shop and put his apron on. "We had quite a run of customers this morning and early afternoon, thanks to you being in jail," he told Shaman. "Folks want ice cream when they're all lathered up about injustice and stuff. We need more drama in this town, I guess." He took Josh and went to join his wife in a booth.

"Why do you ask?" Tempest said.

"I don't know. I just never heard you speak about him. I talk more about my old man than you do about the guy your mom was married to."

She did not look happy. "Well, there's nothing to tell. He was a really handsome man. My mother was crazy about him. It drove her nuts, always waiting on him. He was fair-haired and liked the drink, so he went from town to town getting a job and then getting fired. Mac Cupertino was not one for staying in one place. Or raising a family."

"Hey, that gives me a few points, maybe, huh? I'm not so good-looking, I don't drink very much unless you bring it in the picnic basket, and I'm all over raising a family. You should give me a second look, Cupertino."

She pressed her lips together for an instant, then shook her head. "Let's just stick to the original plan."

"I suggest an extension on the original plan." He'd known this moment was coming. Every time she got close, she skittered away. Like Candy, the wild mustang who wanted to kick him every time he put a lead rope on her. He'd had to watch for those nimble hooves.

Now he had a woman who'd been distinctly nervous ever since he'd put a wedding band on her finger.

"I can't," she said. "I can't make myself believe in fairy tales, Shaman. I know all about make-believe—that's my business, it's what I do. But I just can't make myself trust that you and I will make it for the long haul."

It would be hard to do that if one's supposed "father" had blown in and out of one's life growing up. And that's when he knew he was up against more than just a woman who didn't want to "be married for the sake of the children."

Tempest really didn't understand that a marriage could be something better than emotionally devastating. As she'd said, she didn't believe in fairy tales.

He had a slash across his cheek and a chunk torn out of his shoulder, scars and rough patches all over. There was no make-believe about his life, or him.

She was going to have to learn to believe in herself.

"Look, doll. I'm not that easy to get rid of. I've been in firefights and war zones, and I've hung on many a bronc till the bell. If you don't want to stay married, fine. But you think long and hard about what you're going to tell those boys later on. I am not going to be a dad who blows into their lives from time to time."

She stared at him silently, her eyes wide.

"Think about it," he said. "And when you're ready, you come tell me that you know the man you married is the one who's always going to wake up next to you, look out for you and give you that ride to happily-ever-after. You've got to believe, Tempest, and trust that it will. Or it was over before you ever unpacked that first picnic basket of yours. Whatever it was you were looking for that day you came to my house, only you know. Let me know when you figure it out."

Chapter Fifteen

Shaman headed over to see the sheriff at the jail. It was time to get some answers.

"Oh, no," Nance said, pushing his hat back to glare at him. "I thought I told you to git. This is a jail, not an army barracks."

Shaman smiled. "You may have to let me sleep here. There's no room in the inn in Tempest."

"Not my problem if you got yourself on the hot seat with your woman. When I annoy Mrs. Nance, I'm smart enough to stay out of her way for a while. Then I hit the flower shop on my way home. That's all the advice I have to give you."

Shaman looked around the barren room. There were no pictures or posters, not much of anything on the pale white walls. A small lamp burned on the sheriff's desk. "The ambience of this place isn't bad. Think you could use a green plant, though."

"Thank you, Martha Stewart. What can I do for you?"

Shaman grinned. "I want to know what you're going to do about Bobby Taylor. He has no place to live now. I don't want him making any trouble for my wife."

"I haven't seen him today, so I have no idea what he's going to do now that his rat hole's been destroyed. My best guess would be you watch your back. Bobby doesn't have much use for you, is what I hear."

"Shaman," Tempest said, breezing into the jail.

Both men looked up, surprised.

"Yes, honey bunch?"

She shook her head at him. "Don't sweet-talk me. Ask Sheriff Nance. It doesn't work."

"Not on females who have a decent spirit," the sheriff told Shaman. "And your wife's spirit is pretty super-sized."

"Okay. Yes, Cupertino?" Shaman amended, smiling.

Tempest gave him a don't-push-me glare. "You don't get to just have a meltdown and then walk out. What got into you, soldier?"

"I think it's you," he declared, and the sheriff said, "Always a good answer, cowboy."

"This is not my first rodeo, Sheriff." Shaman looked at his wife. "Tempest, this is what I think. I think you're crazy about me, but I don't think you trust yourself to believe it's real. I think you always dug me a lot, from the very first time you met me, but you're used to glowing reviews in the newspapers, and I'm pretty much that strong, silent type you thought you wanted. That's all I was saying." He smiled at her. "I'm aware that an unemployed ex-soldier isn't what you had in mind for your future husband, but this is the card you've drawn, beautiful."

"Thank you for explaining that," she said. "I'll let you know my answer when I've considered your résumé."

She went out, and Shaman looked at Sheriff Nance.

"You were doing good until you reminded her you were broke." The lawman laughed. "You're supposed to be a prince."

"I am," Shaman said. "I just have other gifts to offer. The size of my wallet is not the thing I'm going to be able to win her with."

"That's too bad. Size does matter."

"I do all right. I saved a lot of what I made in the military. Jonas isn't the tightwad you might think he would be, and I did okay working for him." Shaman looked at Nance. "Maybe you've got an opening for a deputy."

"You lied to an officer of the law," the sheriff reminded him. "Not a quality characteristic."

"I thought my wife had done it. What would you do if you thought Mrs. Nance had suddenly burned down a house?"

"I don't know. I love her. I'd probably build her a new one."

Shaman straightened. "That's a good idea."

"Isn't that what you came in here for? A good idea?"

"Actually," Shaman said, "I came in here to find out if you knew who Tempest's real father is."

The sheriff stared at him. "I have no idea. Some said Bud Taylor, but I never knew if that was so. If you want to know, go to the courthouse and pull her birth records."

"Can I do that?"

"Mrs. McTavish can help you. Tell her you want to see the birth records from that year. Better yet, have Tempest go with you. Make a date of it. I bet you haven't had many of those with your wife."

Shaman hesitated. "Actually, you'd be right."

"This younger generation," Sheriff Nance said with a sigh, "they have no idea of romance. It's all sex, and then—"

"'Bye, Sheriff. Thanks." Shaman headed out of the jail, running smack into Bobby Taylor.

"Hey," Bobby said. "How come you're not locked up? You shouldn't be out."

"I didn't do anything. Nothing to keep me on." Shaman's temper went to red-hot. "Why did you do it?"

The sneaky man appeared openly amused. "Why would I burn down the only place I had to live?"

"Because you have a twisted mind," Shaman retorted. "And because you're determined to hurt Tempest."

"Hey, that sounds almost like you think you know what I'm thinking. However, you don't. Anyway, I need to talk to the sheriff about giving me a cell for the night, since I'm homeless and all."

Shaman grimaced, telling himself that smashing Bobby a good one would get him nowhere but back in Sheriff Nance's unhomey cell. "Good luck with that." He took off toward the flower shop, the sheriff's idea uppermost in his mind.

Heck, I didn't even give her an engagement ring, just a plain gold band when we got married.

He'd start with flowers. That seemed safest.

"WHAT THE HELL IS THAT?" Sheriff Nance demanded two hours after he'd last seen Shaman. A big green spathiphyllum plant hovered in the corner of his office.

Bobby Taylor grinned. "That cowboy soldier brought it. Said you needed a little life in here. I think he's sucking up to you, Sheriff, since his wife burned down my house."

Nance stared at Bobby. "Shaman Phillips left this?"

"Yeah. Said it didn't need much light, but would clean up the air a bit in here. I told you he's crazy, Sheriff."

"Shut up, Bobby, before I have the deputy tape your mouth shut." He eyed the plant. "You ought to be nicer to your sister. She's got someone watching her back now."

Anger crossed the man's face. "He won't always be around."

Sheriff Nance shot his guest a grim glance. "How do you know?"

Bobby smiled. "C'mon, Sheriff. You know very well that Zola'll move on soon enough. When she does, her cowboy soldier'll go back wherever he came from."

"You seem so sure."

Bobby shrugged. "My sister doesn't stay anywhere for long. He knows it as well as anyone. Now that she's burned her house down, she'll probably be gone before you figure out how she did it."

The sheriff frowned at him. "Maybe *you* did it."

Bobby settled more comfortably in his cell, lying down and sighing. "It was all I had, Sheriff. My sister has a house in some fancy place. And she's got Shinny and Blanche's bungalow. Why would I burn down what little I had in this world?"

"To get your sister in trouble. But now you've annoyed her husband, and he'll be keeping an eye on you."

"I don't think so." Taylor smiled as he closed his eyes. "Like I said, he'll go once she runs him off. My sister doesn't keep anyone in her life for very long."

Sheriff Nance turned his gaze back to the spath plant. If it was true that plants could help process bad air into good, maybe he should relocate it.

With his boot, he scooted the big plant in front of Bobby's cell, and then dialed Tempest's cell phone.

"HELLO?" Tempest juggled the babies and some diapers, tucking the phone under her ear. "Hi, Sheriff. How are you and your lovely wife?"

She smiled at her two sons as she laid them on the bed, each giving a tiny protest at being out of her arms. They were so darling, so cute. She was so happy to be a mother.

She didn't know what to do about being a wife. Shaman had made her distinctly uncomfortable with his tempting offer. But she knew he'd never wanted to live here in Tempest for good. Now that she'd seen his home in Hell's Colony—it was a castle, as Cat had claimed—she wondered if he could ever be happy in this one-stoplight town.

"Bobby's here at the jail for the night. He needed a place to sleep," Sheriff Nance told her. "Just thought you'd want to know."

"That's a new one. He burned my house down, and he's sleeping in your jail?"

"Yeah. Can't say much more than that. Just thought you'd want to know, as I said. And your man was in here a minute ago. Not that it's any of my business, but I think he's getting antsy."

She frowned. "Antsy?"

"He's asking a lot of questions about your father," the lawman said.

"Why does he care?"

"I don't know how his mind works. You just might want to be aware. It's never a good thing when a man thinks too much. They almost always come up with the wrong answers."

"Thanks for the tip." Tempest hung up the phone just as banging sounded on her door. "Who is it?"

"Shaman!"

She looked at the babies with a sigh. "That's your daddy, standing on the front porch, yelling at the top of his lungs instead of just opening the door. Come in!"

She heard the front door open and then shut. "I'm back in the bedroom!" she called.

Her heart jumped a bit as she heard him walk down the hall. She finished diapering Josh and then started on Gage. "Excuse us for a moment. We're momentarily disrobed."

He was carrying a huge bouquet of flowers that brought a lovely fragrance into the room. "They're so cute nude. Like cherubs," he stated.

She smiled. "I know. I believe they each have your fine backside."

His brows rose. "Usually people settle for comparing eyes, or looking for Grandpa's nose in the family tree."

"There you go, little Gage," she said, finishing the diapering and snapping up the onesie. "You are now one well-dressed dude."

"I'll say." Shaman sat down next to his two sons and held out the flowers to her. "Sheriff Nance says I suck at romance."

She smiled and took the bouquet. "I never expected romance from you, so I'm not disappointed in the least. Not that I totally agree with Tempest's finest."

Shaman didn't appear to like that too well. "How do you think of me?"

"I just told you. You have a great backside. I think my sons may have been fortunate to have inherited it. Watch the boys for a moment, please."

He followed her, toting the babies in his big arms, watching her as she put the flowers in a vase. "Listen, I can't stay. I just came by to tell you that I finally figured out what the problem is."

She looked at him, suddenly wary. "If you know what any problem is, do feel free to share."

"I keep telling you we should stay married. I keep saying we're staying together for the sake of the kids." He kissed one son on the head, then the other. "But then I realized that's not the right thing to do. I know you don't want to stay married to me. I shouldn't try to force you to stay. We had an agreement. I'll stick to it."

She shoved the flowers into the vase and filled it with water. "That's quite a change of heart."

"Yeah. Well, I'm pigheaded. I know it."

She wiped up the water on the counter, trying not to look at him as she gathered her wild thoughts. "Why were you asking questions about my father?"

"Oh." He shrugged. "Because I don't think Bud Taylor was your father. I think it was Mac Cupertino. I was hoping if I could prove that, it would give you some closure. Then maybe you'd feel better about settling down with me."

She blinked. "You think I don't want to be married to you because I don't know who my father is?"

"I think it doesn't help."

"Has it ever occurred to you that maybe a sexual relationship doesn't translate into a committed, love-for-all-time marriage just because it results in babies?"

He sat down on the sofa across the room, looking dreamy in worn jeans and a dark shirt. "I know. I know those things worry you. And you've got this crazy brother running around trying to kill everything you love, which can't be easy."

"Don't worry about me, soldier. I can handle myself."

"Yeah, but you're an actress," Shaman said, winning himself no points with her at the moment. She was beginning to steam. "What do you know about taking care of yourself? Still, I think you'll be fine from now on. Taylor knows everyone's watching him. Plus you're making new friends in the town, and have a storytelling and theater class gig." He gazed at her, more handsome than any man should be. "You don't need me anymore."

She stared at him. "Don't I?"

"Pretty sure you never did." Shaman shrugged. "I'm just saying, I don't want you to feel forced to stay with me. Marriage isn't for wimps."

"I'll say." She wasn't thrilled with her husband at the moment. "So, are you trying to slither off on me? On us?"

"I want you to be happy," Shaman said.

She put her hands on her hips, thoroughly disgusted with him. "I want *you* to be happy."

"I'd be happy," Shaman said, "if I was in bed with you. That's when I was happiest."

She hesitated. The hours she'd spent in Shaman's arms had made her happy, too. In fact, they were the happiest she'd ever been. "I don't think that would solve anything right now."

"I don't know," Shaman said. "I do pretty good convincing when I'm naked with you."

It was true.

"It can't be just about that. A relationship has to be built on more than sex."

"Pretty sure I'm fine with a relationship built on sex," Shaman said. "I'm not a needy kind of guy."

She wouldn't let herself smile. "Shaman, I never thanked you for trying to save me from going to jail. Even though it was unnecessary, and my boys do not need their father in prison, I do appreciate you trying to help."

He sighed. "Actually, I was being selfish. The boys need to be fed and looked after, and besides, the gossip in this town would never cease. For the rest of their lives, the twins would hear about their jailbird mother. I was not going to let that happen."

She sat down next to him and the babies, touching her hand to each child's head. "It's nice to know you're looking out for me. I like that about you almost better than your lovemaking."

The expression on his face was comical. "Then I haven't made love to you satisfactorily, Cupertino. And I'm a minus in the romance department, according to the sheriff. I've got some things to fix."

"Maybe romance isn't measured in flowers. Maybe Sheriff Nance only knows about Mrs. Nance, and not all women. Maybe women are not one-size-fits-all."

He looked at her, his expression a bit hopeful.

"I happen to think that a man who will go to jail for me is a bit of a hero. And that's very romantic," Tempest said. She leaned over and kissed him on the cheek. "It just occurred to me that we haven't made love since we got married, soldier."

Shaman looked distinctly tempted, and very wolfish. She felt a shiver run over her.

"It has been a long time."

It was on the tip of her tongue to agree. And yet, to what purpose? He wasn't in love with her. If it hadn't been for the babies, she doubted he'd be in Tempest right now.

"Anyway," Shaman said, "I just wanted to let you know that I'm going back to Hell's Colony. Xav has come out of his coma, and I need to go help Kendall keep an eye on him. Gage is going, too, but he really needs to be at Rancho Diablo with Cat until she finishes school."

Tempest's heart nearly stopped. "When are you leaving?"

"Probably after we put the boys to bed for the night." He touched each baby gently. "I think it's best."

He meant that it would be best for him to go, without her. "Is this because of Bobby?" she asked. "You going to jail, and being accused of arson?"

"I don't care much about that."

She didn't believe him. He'd gotten his head split open like a grape, and so had his brother, and then he'd been in jail. Because of her, because of Bobby. "That's why you were trying to find out who my father was. You know that if Bud Taylor was truly my family, you'll always be tied to Bobby." She was sad for her boys, and sad for herself. "I don't blame you. You deserve a more decent family tree."

"I only looked up your birth records because Blanche was sort of hinting around that you and Bobby weren't related." He shrugged. "Cupertino, I couldn't care less who your family is. My hope was that if you weren't related to Bobby, you could tell him to buzz off."

"It won't work," she said. "He's mad about the money." She straightened. "So who was my father?"

"Mac Cupertino," Shaman said. "That's what's on the birth records."

"Oh." Tempest's heart flipped over. "Then why did Bud leave me his money?"

"Could be that he really loved your mother. We know he didn't care for his relations, and if Bobby is a representative sample, maybe I can see why. You'll probably never know."

"It doesn't matter now." She looked down at the boys, who were snoozing next to each other, between her and Shaman. "I didn't want anything of Mr. Taylor's."

"Yeah. I hope you're okay with the news. You gonna be all right?"

"I'm fine," she said quickly. "It's actually good news."

He nodded. "Well, I'd best hit the road. Need to go thank my sister for sending the heavy artillery on my behalf." Shaman leaned over and kissed her on the cheek, but it didn't feel like the kisses he'd given her in the early days of their relationship. "I'll call you soon enough and check on the boys."

She was starting to get annoyed with her big cowboy. How dense could he be? "Just because we may not extend our agreement doesn't mean…"

"Doesn't mean what, Cupertino?" he asked, his voice soft.

"I don't know." She wrapped a blanket around the boys, just to have something to do with her hands. It was so hard to look in Shaman's eyes. "Thank you for the flowers. They're lovely."

"Thanks for coming to sit in jail with me." He grinned at her, a rascal to the very end, a rascal who seemed determined to carry off her heart. "It's a memory I'm sure we'll look back on and treasure."

"Tell Xav and Kendall and Millicent hello. From me and the boys."

He smiled again, then picked up her hand, kissing it. "You're a beautiful mother, Cupertino. Definitely the beauty in the fairy tale."

She watched as he kissed his boys, then got up from the sofa, put his hat on, walked to the front door. "Take care of yourself."

She nodded. "You, too."

"Lock the door." He left, and her heart jumped almost painfully in her chest. She put a hand over her breast, willing herself to calm down.

His truck started, then lights flashed in the window as he pulled away from the adobe bungalow. She looked down at her children, who were sleeping peacefully, unaware that their father had just left their mother.

Somehow, it felt so much like history repeating itself that it opened up a hollow place inside her.

She got up and locked the door.

Chapter Sixteen

Back in his brother's bedroom at the spacious family compound Shaman was relieved. Shaman hadn't realized just how responsible he'd felt in this whole situation. His little brother shouldn't have suffered for his sake.

When Xav opened his eyes, Shaman breathed a sigh of relief. "Hey."

"Hey." He smiled wanly. "What are you doing here?"

"Came to see if you'd joined the living."

"Barely." Xav reached for the water bottle on his nightstand. "What hit me?"

"The testing hasn't come back, but I suspect a lead pipe."

"Thank God," Xav said, sipping his water. "I was afraid it was something dumb, like I'd let a door blow open on me or something."

"No." Shaman shook his head. "The same wacko that attacked me got to you. You just got it worse than I did."

"Yeah, I guess so." Xav winced. "They tell me I had surgery for swelling."

"They were going to, but the swelling subsided. You got lucky, bro." Anger flashed through Shaman all over again, seething and roiling. He leaned back in the leather armchair. "Millicent says you'll be fine in a few days."

"Yeah. I'm feeling much better now that it doesn't seem like I can pick up radio stations in Chicago from the ringing in my ears." Xav smiled. "Do they know who was on the other end of the lead pipe?"

He nodded. "Tempest's half brother Bobby Taylor. He's got a bit of a grudge against her. Only, the late-breaking news is that they're not related at all, which further complicates things. She doesn't want anyone to know that Bobby's father, Bud, who owned Dark Diablo before Jonas bought it, left her his entire estate and holdings. It seems to be a problem for Bobby."

Xav blinked. "That's a tangled web."

"Tell me about it."

"So when did Jonas buy Dark Diablo from Bud Taylor?"

"About two years ago. Then the old guy died. It was like he was waiting to get rid of it." Shaman grimaced. "From what I can tell, he sold out and lived in the farmhouse until he croaked. That was the deal he and Jonas made."

Xav moved restlessly. "He must have believed Tempest was his daughter."

Shaman shrugged. "Maybe he felt guilty for not helping her out when she was a kid. She grew up pretty poor."

"And Bobby had no idea he had a half sister?"

"He knew. He just didn't think the embarrassment of his life—Tempest—was going to make off with the family riches."

Shaman considered the vast wealth Tempest had doled out in the small town. "She got rid of all the dough, parceling it out to different places. Anonymously. The library got the lion's share. Then Millicent offered a wedding gift to us, and my bride generously had Mother make a donation—anonymously—to the elementary school."

"You have a philanthropic wife." Xav considered his words. "But she's not Bobby's sister?"

Shaman shrugged. "Not according to her birth records. She's Mac Cupertino's daughter. Apparently, her mother loved him, couldn't resist him. He just wasn't much for hanging around, so I guess that's why she took up with Bud Taylor."

"But her mother passed Tempest off as Bud's kid."

Shaman blinked. "That never crossed my mind."

Xav grinned. "You're the family valedictorian."

"Yeah." The pieces fell into place for him. "That explains why Bud left her the money. He really believed Tempest was his child. If Bobby knew that she wasn't in fact his half sister, he'd really be hot." Thankfully, no one knew that information except him and the sheriff, and Tempest. Maybe Shinny and Blanche.

"And you're sitting here why?" Xav asked.

Shaman looked at his brother. "Because Kendall and Millicent can't do everything for you while you lie around like a Roman god."

"I meant," Xav said patiently, "why are you sitting here if Bobby Taylor's got a reason to be even more angry? Once he finds out Tempest isn't his sister, he's going to figure out what her mother did. All this time he's been ticked at Jonas for buying the place—taking advantage of his daddy's advanced age, wasn't that his story? Now he's got a real target with a face and a name. His not-blood-relation, Tempest."

Shaman's blood chilled. He stared at his brother,

thinking about his wife alone with their two children, and a madman out for vengeance watching their every move.

"I've got to go," he said.

Xav nodded. "You sure do."

Shaman ran out the door, hoping—praying—he hadn't left Tempest and his boys in danger.

"I DON'T KNOW, Jack." Tempest looked at her agent as she pushed the pram over to the courthouse. Two cameramen followed her every move, setting her and the babies up for a commercial for diapers. Jack was determined to keep her working, and Tempest was equally determined to be a stay-at-home mom. For the moment, they'd found a compromise.

But Jack wasn't here to oversee the shoot. He wanted to dangle the prize of a made-for-TV movie in front of her. All she needed to do was take a screen test— although he was certain she had it in the bag.

Tempest didn't want to do a movie. But Blanche had pointed out that someone had to pay her bills, if she was going to be a single mom. Tempest's response was that she'd sell her villa in Tuscany. She and the boys wouldn't need that much to live on in Tempest.

But then Blanche had opined that what she needed was a steady income, especially if she was going to fall for a retired military operative who was out of a job at the moment. "I guess I could do it," Tempest said, thinking that she didn't care if she lived on soup and crackers if it meant that Shaman was in her bed every night.

"That's the spirit," Jack said. Her fair-haired agent grinned. "I knew if I saw you in person I could make you see the wisdom of putting away college money for these little panhandlers."

She smiled. "Jack, I saved my money. I would be fine."

"Can always be finer." He glanced around, taking in the courthouse and the wide streets around the square, the many shops that jutted cheerful signage from their windows and awnings. "This is a quaint part of the world, but I don't see you living here."

Jack didn't understand all the changes the town had undergone just in the past couple of months. This sleepy place was coming to life, as if it had been dormant for most of its existence, and was now waking up to its potential. "I love it here."

"It makes my skin itch. I need action."

A handycam zipped around them, recording Tempest and the babies for the commercial. She stopped on her mark and lifted a baby out of the pram, then the other one. Like veterans, Josh and Gage waved their chubby arms, reaching for their mother.

And the commercial was done.

"Easy money," Jack said.

"I guess so." Tempest was still thinking about the made-for-TV movie. She didn't see Shaman hanging around film studios. He'd be just as crazy and bored as Jack was here, only Shaman's skin wouldn't just "itch" from boredom; he'd be a caged panther. "I'll think about the movie, Jack. Give me a day or two."

He looked at her steadily. "You want to take this deal. These boys are going to want to take dates to proms, even in this hick town. They're going to need braces and—"

"Rodeo gear," Tempest said. "Their father wants them to rodeo."

"Funny thing, for the fifteen years I've been your agent, never have you said the words *rodeo* or *small town*."

"I know." She hugged her sons to her, then handed little Josh carefully to her agent. "Here, Uncle Jack wants to hold you."

"The things I do for you," he grumbled, clasping the baby at arm's length. "I think he has a poo issue."

Tempest laughed and took Josh back, placing him next to his brother in the pram. "You know, these guys are only going to be little for a few years. I think I—"

"I'm going to go finish up with the director, see if there's anything else he needs before you say that being a mother is all you want to do. I hear it coming," Jack stated. "And I'm pretty sure you'd look back on that decision and regret it. You're right on the cusp of your career getting huge, Tempest."

He handed her the diaper bag he'd been carrying, and hurried off. She smiled down tenderly at her sons. "Poo issue, indeed." The boys were both clean and dry, although they looked as if they might want to eat soon. She rolled them over to a bench outside the courthouse and sat down, popping open a couple of bottles and starting to feed them.

It was so peaceful and quiet in Tempest. She had everything she wanted—except her marriage. And she really wasn't certain what to do about that.

"Hey," Bobby Taylor said, sitting down next to her on the bench.

He could not have missed that she was annoyed by his presence, since she gave him her sternest frown. "What do you want?"

"Nothing." He looked down at the babies, then glanced around the courthouse lawn, his gaze searching. "Where's Captain Courageous?"

She ignored that, her pulse beating faster. They were in a shadowy corner out of the sun, where not many people walked by. Jack would be back in a minute, but he wouldn't be in a hurry to return, either. He was much more comfortable talking shtick with producers than he was playing Uncle Jack, even if he had bought her the pretty diaper bag from Hollywood.

"Go away, Bobby. I'm busy."

He considered the babies. "Don't look much like the cowboy."

She didn't bother to even glance at him. "I don't expect them to look like anybody except themselves right now."

He reached out to touch one of the infants. Tempest slapped his hand away. "Take off, Bobby."

She stared him down. He glared back at her.

"Figured you might be nice without the cowboy around," he told her. "Guess I was wrong."

"Yes. You are." She put the babies back in the pram. They didn't appreciate being separated from their bottles, so they set up a nice, healthy squalling. Bobby skittered off like a cockroach, wending his way around the back of the courthouse.

"Whew," Jack said, coming to find her. "I can hear them a half mile away. Maybe I can find them a commercial for baby aspirin or something. I can feel a headache coming on."

"Two little babies don't make as much noise as you do in five minutes, Jack." Tempest wheeled the stroller toward the Ice Cream Shoppe. "You're a sneaky agent, Jack. But I'll do the movie."

"Great!" He radiated a let's-hit-the-road-before-you-change-your-mind smile. "Can you leave today?"

WHEN SHAMAN OPENED THE door to the bungalow with the key Shinny had given him at Tempest's request, he was shocked to find the place almost empty. The port-a-cribs were up against a wall, the place was vacuumed, all baby paraphernalia was gone.

"Shaman!" Blanche entered the bungalow, her high hairdo tottering as she hurried.

"Hi, Blanche." He glanced around. "Do you know where Tempest is?"

"She took the boys and went to Hollywood with her agent. They shot a commercial here—you should have seen it, it was so neat to have a TV crew in Tempest— and then she left. She's making a made-for-TV movie." Blanche glowed with pride. "She tried to call you, but your cell wasn't working. Or it wouldn't pick up."

They did get faulty cell service on occasion out at The Family, Inc., a feature of being far from the nearest towns and cell towers. He checked his phone, finding about ten messages and texts from Tempest. His heart sank a bit.

"She said she left you a note in the kitchen." Blanche grinned at him. "Now that the boys have been in a commercial, no doubt they'll grow up on the big screen, if they turn out as handsome as their daddy." She winked at him, and he tried to wash away the sense of panic enveloping him.

"Thanks, Blanche." He gazed around the bungalow once more, feeling lost and bereft without his wife and boys. That was the problem: he thought of Tempest as his wife. She still thought of their relationship as an agreement. Like any other contract she signed.

"So, are you going to stay awhile?" Blanche asked. "I'm sure Tempest wouldn't mind you being here."

This was Tempest's bungalow. He hadn't seen their lives so clearly cut into his-and-hers before. Except for the babies, they had nothing that was *theirs*.

"I guess I'll be moving on."

The older woman looked at him, her broad, friendly face creased with concern. "Are you all right?"

He nodded. "I'm fine."

"If it makes you feel any better, I think Bobby's not going to try to kill you anymore. He says he's turning over a new leaf. He's even been helping out at Cactus Max's, washing dishes in exchange for meals."

Shaman couldn't say why that didn't necessarily make him feel better. But maybe he was just sad that his wife didn't seem to want to be married to him anymore.

And the fact was, he really couldn't blame her.

Blanche left after a few more pleasantries, and then he went over to read Tempest's letter. It told him where she and the boys were staying, invited him to come out and join them. Said she wasn't sure how long he'd planned to be in Hell's Colony, and hadn't been able to get hold of him. That she showed the boys his picture every night and told them their daddy was a good man, which made him smile because his tiny sons cared about nothing at this stage except being held, eating and having their diapers changed.

He put the letter away and walked outside, surprised when he saw Gage and Chelsea drive up with Cat. They parked at the back of Shinny's. His niece hopped out of the truck, flying over to throw her arms around him.

"Uncle Shaman! We knew we'd find you here! Dad says that the Ice Cream Shoppe has become your favorite haunt."

He sent his brother a grimace. "Thanks, Gage."

Then he realized his sister-in-law was carrying something long and white in a protective bag. He pounded his brother on the back in greeting, keeping a wary eye on Chelsea and her big smile. "Where's my tiny niece?"

"Abigail Catherine stayed with Fiona." Chelsea's face positively glowed with excitement, and he had a funny feeling his sister-in-law had something on her mind. She wore that pleased look Tempest used to wear when she was about to spring something on him. Way back when it used to be a picnic basket and sex.

He missed those days. Now she was still springing things on him, but it was usually the theory that their marriage contract had expired. Definitely less sex—make that no sex—and, coincidentally, no picnic basket.

He sighed. "I hope that is not for me."

Chelsea held up the long garment bag, which was rather voluminous, so it must not contain a simple baby gift of matching onesies for the boys. "This is for Tempest. If she wants it."

She marched past him into the bungalow. Shaman's gaze met his brother's. Gage shrugged. "Something about magic," he muttered.

"You could use some magic, Uncle Shaman," Cat said, looking up at him. "Chelsea says that if Tempest has gone back to being an actress, you're probably going to need to marry her right."

He glanced over at his sister-in-law, who raised her shoulders in a delicate shrug.

"Most of the Callahan brides have needed two times at the altar. I think it cements the love that was already there, but goes unrecognized in the epic struggle of a man meeting his match," she said.

Gage smiled, not offended in the least and clearly agreeing with his wife. "It's not as bad as it sounds, bro."

"Aunt Fiona says you probably want to get married at Rancho Diablo," Cat said. "She says you probably would feel better having your vows said by someone other than an Elvis impersonator and his pink-haired wife. Not that it was bad, Uncle Shaman, but as weddings go, it probably wasn't special." She smiled at her uncle. "It was cool, but not fairy tale."

"I don't think Tempest would marry me again."

"You don't know unless you ask, do you?" Chelsea said.

He looked around the bungalow yet again, feeling out of place with the problem he found himself facing. "Our lives intersect. They don't align or combine."

"Yeah." Gage nodded. "You probably want to fix that, bro."

He wasn't going to say he'd tried, because even he wasn't certain he'd done anything but attempt to figure out how to survive Bobby and keep his family safe. "I guess I had my mind on other things."

"Being a new dad is tough," Gage commiserated. "I did it for a teen and now a baby. I can't tell you which one was more challenging. But it's all fun." He pulled his daughter to him for a squeeze, which she returned joyfully.

"I don't know," Cat said. "Uncle Shaman, you should definitely ask Tempest to marry you again. That way, maybe she'd stay with you."

He wanted that more than anything. But what if she wanted a career and bright lights and applause? He was just a cowboy, a working man. "I don't know," he said, glancing at the long wedding dress twinkling in its clear plastic bag. "She's been through a lot of changes lately. I don't know where I fit in anymore."

"Well," Cat said, "Dad always says no time like the present. Course, he's usually talking about me doing my homework." She smiled up at her father. "We have to go now, Uncle Shaman. Dad and Chelsea are going to let me check out some books from the library. There's one there that's a specially bound edition of Shakespeare's play *The Tempest*. I read it last summer, but want to read it again for my final school project. 'What's Past Is Present,' is what I'm going to call it. Cool, huh?"

He smiled at his niece. "It is cool. Chelsea, I don't think I need the dress. You can take it back to Rancho Diablo." He kissed his sister-in-law. "Thanks for thinking of us, but I think our problems go way beyond what a dress can fix."

"I wouldn't diss the dress," Gage said. "You'd be surprised how these ladies love to jump into that thing. It's supposedly charmed. And as long as my girl sees me as her Prince Charming, I call that a beautiful gown."

Shaman smiled. "Thanks for stopping by."

"Are you going out to California?" Chelsea asked.

"Actually, no. I'm not." Shaman glanced one last time at the dress, and then at the empty port-a-cribs. "I'm going to swing by a lawyer's office and see about beginning divorce proceedings."

WHAT HE'D FIGURED OUT—and maybe he was slow—was that if Cupertino wanted their marriage to work, she'd be with him. The boys were all they had that linked them.

It seemed it wasn't going to be enough.

"She could have called here," he told Kendall.

"We do have land lines and company phone lines," his sister mused. "But I don't know that she has those numbers."

"Cupertino's resourceful. She could have found me, let me know she was going. This is the thing about my wife—she doesn't want to be married to me."

"Yeah, I guess." Kendall looked at him as they sat around Xav's bed. "But you don't want to have the family legal beagles start proceedings, Shaman. You don't really want a divorce."

"It's true. But it's time to move on."

"I don't like it," Xav said. "I mean, it's your life, but I don't know that I took a lead pipe to the back of my head for the woman you love, just to turn her loose."

His brother looked better, human again.

"What are you doing when you get clearance from the doctor to get out of that bed?" Shaman asked.

Xav smiled. "Well, we weren't going to tell you today, but Kendall and I have some news for you."

"Make it good news."

Kendall couldn't contain a face-splitting smile. "Xav's decided to return to Dark Diablo."

Shaman raised a brow. "Decided you like foreman work?"

Xav nodded. "I really do like doing things outside. It's a huge change from The Family, Inc., and I need it."

"And I'm joining him." Kendall and her twin shared a conspiratorial grin. "Xav's not the only one who gets to listen for spirit owls, though I still think that's just guy talk for communing with nature without any responsibilities." She looked pleased with her jab at her brothers. "Jonas has hired me to redecorate. I have an almost open budget, because he wants everything to be fabulous, and I do fabulous well," she said gleefully. "And when he starts building his hospital, I can help him with that, too. It's a dream come true."

Shaman blinked. "What about The Family, Inc.? What about Millicent?"

"Millicent is fine. She and Fitzgerald want to travel. We're going to base Gil Phillips, Inc., out of Dark Diablo until Jonas gets the new house built. We can work just about anywhere these days."

"New house?"

Kendall smiled. "Jonas wants something pretty identical to Rancho Diablo. He's wanted that for a long time. And I get the decorating and overseeing of that project, too."

"You are going to be busy." Which would suit his brother and sister just fine. Kendall was never happier than when she had about ninety projects going. "Am I the only Phillips Jonas didn't offer a job to?"

Kendall shrugged. "He figured you'd head out to find your kids. And your wife."

Shaman leaned back in the leather chair. What was keeping him from doing that very thing?

Fear of rejection.

"I don't think I handle rejection well," he said.

Xav shook his head. "You're a decorated soldier. Pretty sure rejection is not the scariest thing you've ever faced."

When you were madly in love with one of the world's most beautiful women, it was probably worse than a year spent eating MREs. "She might not want me in California with her."

"Sure she does," Kendall said. "Someone's got to watch the boys while she's on set."

Shaman looked at his sister. "I just want to point out that I don't see you at Dark Diablo. I thought you hated everything about it."

"It grew on me." Kendall laughed at his raised brow. "I like the people, I like the town."

His world was being turned inside out. "What about Bobby? I don't think I like the idea of my baby sister being out there where he can take a whack at you."

"Bought him off," Kendall said. "He gets a monthly stipend from me, as long as he works or volunteers forty hours a week and checks in once a week with Sheriff Nance. It's all in an airtight contract. And since he's sleeping at the jail for now, there probably won't be any problems."

"You bought him off?" Shaman stared at her.

She shrugged, and Xav laughed. "All he wanted was money," Kendall explained. "I know he's a loser and a criminal, but he's a busy loser criminal now. And I feel much safer about my nephews. It's our wedding gift to you, since we never got you one. And we'll be safer, too, because Bobby's not about to mess up his gravy train. Sheriff Nance approved of the idea. Says it's always better to rehabilitate than incarcerate when possible. So we're giving this a shot. We think it'll work."

Shaman shook his head. "You bought off the man who tried to smash my head and Xav's like coconuts. The tests came back conclusive for both our DNA on that lead pipe, you know."

"I wasn't going to let him get at mine," she stated. "Frankly, I work hard to be beautiful."

He wondered if there was anything his sister didn't think she could solve, then decided there wasn't. "I'm game for anything that keeps Bobby away from my family."

"You're welcome," Kendall said. "So back to the divorce proceeding idea… I'm going to vote no."

"It's not your marriage, Kendall. This is the one thing you can't control." Shaman wished Tempest loving him was as easy as letting his sister direct the action.

"Those papers Millicent had her sign were a prenup," Xav interjected.

"I know that." Shaman didn't need to be reminded.

"I think that was part of the problem," Kendall mused. "You should have told Mother no. You should have told her that being with Tempest was your top and only priority. Those papers put your marriage on a business footing from the start."

"I'm going now," Shaman said, annoyed that his siblings didn't seem to remember that he'd done everything he could to woo his wife. He'd married her; he'd tried to protect her. And she kept leaving him.

"She's afraid," Kendall said. "She's afraid of being that sad little girl who lived in that run-down house, with no friends and a dysfunctional family."

Shaman let his sister's words wash over him. "I don't think my wife is afraid of anything. Congratulations on your new jobs." He got up, kissed his sister on the forehead, gave Xav's shoulder a squeeze. "I'm heading out."

"Where are you going now?"

He didn't know. The farmhouse he'd called home for a year was no longer his. Tempest's bungalow was not his home. And neither was Hell's Colony, because he had never wanted it to be.

But Tempest had been happy here.

She'd left only because she wanted to be with him.

He'd forgotten how to be patient. He'd wanted all the answers right away, instead of knowing that the way to cure the past was with patience.

"I may stay here," Shaman said, and Kendall and Xav stared at him.

"Mother would be thrilled," Kendall declared. "She might faint dead away when you tell her, but she'd be delighted. There's a thousand things we need help with. We could use a representative. Like what Xav used to do, until he decided he wanted to play cowboy. You'd be a great rep, especially if you cut that hair. You look like you're about to ride away bareback on that bossy mustang you call Candy."

He laughed. "Candy is not bossy. She's a baby doll, and I learned a lot from her. She taught me patience, which I forgot. Now I'm going to get it back."

He went out the door, whistling.

If the past was a prologue, as Cat said, then the future should be a helluva good book.

He just had to turn the page.

Chapter Seventeen

Shaman liked California, but he wasn't certain about movie sets. Watching Tempest act was a bit of a wacky experience. She'd covered up that beautiful blond hair he loved and was wearing a black wig that hugged her face—he hoped it was a wig or he was going to cry. He couldn't tell from here, but it looked as if she was wearing brown contacts, another change from the baby blues he loved gazing into. She was in the middle of a scene, so he watched, wondering how he could ever fit into her world.

She'd done a much better job of fitting into his than he could in hers.

The man in the scene was dressed like a doctor and had long, raffish brown hair—clearly the leading man. He kissed Tempest, his arms around her, holding her tight, and Shaman thought his blood pressure was going to pop out the top of his head. His heartbeat raced a mile a minute, his throat dried out, his brain felt as if it short-circuited.

This sucked. Compared to all the fear he'd ever felt in a war zone, seeing Tempest in another man's arms just about knocked him to his knees. He told himself that this was pretend, this was make-believe—but it was also her life, and that was going to be hard for him to roll with.

He'd never really believed he had her, that she was his. In his mind, she was always the beauty beyond his reach, while he was beaten up, stripped of some of life's better emotions.

She had given him those emotions back. Joy, hope, longing.

He didn't think he could hang around watching her kiss good-looking dudes, though. Even he could tell the actor enjoying his wife's sweet lips was no booby prize in the dating pond.

Tempest reared back and slapped the doctor, and suddenly Shaman felt a whole lot better. They went on speaking their parts, and his blood pressure calmed, his fight-or-flight response quit trying to strangle him.

Then the scene was over and the lights came up. People started walking around the constructed set, and Shaman wondered how anybody could spend long days inside a box like this, in a fishbowl with cameras and people peering at them.

This was not for him. He belonged outside, working with his hands, building things. Breathing fresh air.

"Hey," the director yelled. "Tempest! You got a visitor!"

Shaman straightened, his heart hammering as she looked around, then walked over to him.

"Shaman! You made it!"

As if she'd never doubted that he would. He cheered up a bit.

"Yeah. I made it."

"What do you think?" She flung her hand to indicate

the set, and Shaman realized she was proud of her work, just as he was proud of his.

"I'm glad it's your job and not mine," he said. "I'm not good at playing make-believe. I never was. Ask Xav and Kendall."

She smiled at him. "I'm not surprised. You've never been one for suspense. Come on, I want to show you something."

"I wouldn't say I don't like suspense," Shaman said, following his wife gladly. He'd missed her so much it was as if he'd had a hole inside ever since he'd talked to the lawyers about divorcing her. His heart had been leaking like an hourglass, and now he was with her, but he wasn't certain at all if she wanted their marriage to last or not.

She was right. He was no good with suspense.

"Look." Tempest pulled him into a room where two cribs and a playpen were set up. Gage and Josh were in the playpen, holding soft stuffed animals. A babysitter sat beside it, smiling at the babies. "This is Dana. She's awesome with the boys. Dana, this is my husband, Shaman."

"Hi," Dana said.

"I'm done filming for today. You can go, Dana. Thank you for your help."

"I love watching them!" the teen exclaimed. "They're the best. Nice to meet you, Shaman." She grabbed her purse and went off.

Shaman felt immensely hopeful that Tempest had introduced him as her husband. He took Josh out of the playpen and kissed him, then did the same with little Gage. "If you're done filming for the day, does that mean you can lose the wig? I'm really hoping that's a wig."

She nodded. "It's a wig."

"I mean, you're beautiful this way, too," Shaman said, "but I fell for you as a blonde. And I never was much for make-believe, as I said."

She smiled at him. "You're a salt-of-the-earth guy, Shaman. It's one of the things that attracted me to you in the beginning."

He didn't like the sound of that; wasn't she attracted to him now? "Yeah, well, it can be boring, I guess."

Tempest looked at him. "How is the family?"

He recognized a change of subject when he heard it. "Xav is on the mend. He and Kendall are going to work at Dark Diablo. With Xav, I understand, but Kendall, never."

Tempest went to a mirror, pulled off the wig, began scrubbing at her makeup. Shaman was relieved to see his wife reappearing.

"I'm not surprised," she said. "Dark Diablo is the kind of place where people figure out what they want in life."

He eyed his wife with great interest as she began shucking her costume. He didn't want a divorce, he wanted Tempest. Here in California or in Tempest or even in Hell's Colony, he really didn't care.

"Hey," Shaman said. "I could hang out in California while you film, watch the boys. You know, be a full-time dad."

She turned to gaze at him, her eyes wide. "Are you serious?"

Was he? Of course he was. He shrugged. "I'm a pretty easygoing guy."

"You are not," Tempest said.

"I'm trying to be," Shaman countered.

She gave him a long look. "What about us?"

"Well," he said, not exactly certain how to answer a question that was about to kill him. "I guess you want a divorce."

He thought her face fell just a little. But she was still wearing those darn brown contacts, so it was throwing him off a bit.

"Can you take out the contacts? I miss your eyes," he said.

She smiled, turned back to the mirror and popped them out. He walked over and sat down next to her, shifting the babies so that they were comfortable in his lap. "That's better," he said. "See? There's your mommy, boys."

Tempest shook her head. "Did you come here to ask for a divorce?"

"No," Shaman said. "I came here to find my wife. For that matter, I came here to try to keep my wife. I'm trying to square your job with my understanding of life. It's not going to be easy to watch you smooching skinny actor dudes with gel in their hair, but I can suck it up." He shrugged. "Well, I can handle it infrequently. Not every day. I have only so much goodness in my soul."

She leaned over and put her lips on his. "The only way I get through the kisses on set is by imagining that it's you."

He pulled back to look at her, searching her eyes for her real feelings. "So, what happens after this gig?"

She looked at him. "You tell me, soldier."

He wasn't sure. But something—that sense of timing he relied on—was telling him he was headed into safe water, that everything was going to be good. He could actually win the princess, if he was a changed beast. "I love you, Tempest. Zola Cupertino. I'm madly in love with you and have been since the moment you walked into my life. You gave me sons I adore, and you make me want to spend every day of my life making you smile. If you want a divorce, I'll go along with it just to make you happy." He took a deep breath. "But if it's up to me, I'd rather have a real wedding. A big, wonderland wedding with all our friends and family around to see me make the most wonderful woman in the world my wife. I'm talking amazing. Because that's what you are to me."

Tempest's eyes sparkled with joy. "I've dreamed of being a real wife to you, Shaman. One with no strings attached."

"And no contracts," Shaman said. "No prenups. We're together, all in, you and me. And these little tigers. I want to build you a house for a wedding gift, to replace the one you had. A big house, where we can have plenty of kids. And a media room, so the kids can watch their mother's movies."

"I would love a house you build for me. Thank you, Shaman. It's a wonderful wedding gift." Tempest's heart swelled with happiness and love. She smiled at him. "Want to hear a secret?"

"Sure." Although there had been enough secrets they'd had to dig through to be together. He hoped this one was a good secret.

"If you didn't ask me, I was going to propose to you."

"Really." He perked up, feeling as if he'd caught the moon. "I would have said yes, beautiful."

She kissed him again, a little longer this time. "And I'm saying yes, soldier."

The babies squirmed between them, and Tempest

smiled down at her sons, taking one from Shaman. With one hand now free, Shaman framed Tempest's face with his palm and gave her a kiss nothing like the one the fake doctor had given her.

"Wow," she said, "if that's the way you're going to kiss me when we're really married, I'm going to be a very happy wife." She peered at him. "Are we really going to do this?"

He kissed her again, making certain she had no doubt about his intentions.

"I think that's a yes," she said breathlessly.

Shaman smiled. "And I hear there's a magic wedding dress that's been offered, if that's of any interest to you. I don't know if you believe in magic."

Tempest leaned her head against Shaman's. "All my life, I dreamed of being swept away by a handsome prince. And now it's happening." She kissed him with her whole heart. "I believe in magic every time you hold me."

Shaman held his wife and his babies to him. From beast to prince... He was the happiest man on earth.

Soldier, husband, father. It was all about family.

Happily ever after.

Epilogue

Three months later, after filming wrapped

The magic wedding dress fitted Tempest the way she always dreamed her wedding dress would. It fell in soft folds around her, shimmering and luminous, and she held her breath every time she glanced in the mirror.

"Did you see him?" Cat asked, her little face shining with delight.

"Who?" Tempest asked, pretending she didn't know about the legend of the gown's magic. "Did I see who?"

"The man of your dreams, Aunt Tempest!" Cat seemed as if she could barely stand the excitement. She looked darling in a long, sky-blue dress, feeling very important because she got to be a junior bridesmaid.

Chelsea, her matron of honor, gazed at Tempest. "Did you?" she asked. "I will admit that I didn't really believe in the magic wedding gown, but I definitely saw my true love once I put it on."

Tempest was very familiar with the world of make-believe and fairy tales. She smiled at Kendall, her maid of honor, and the others. "Of course I did. But then, I saw him in Las Vegas, too."

She'd always known that Shaman was the only man

for her. Maybe she'd tried to ignore it, and maybe she hadn't thought she deserved a man as wonderful as him.

"I can't wait for my turn to wear the magic wedding dress," Cat said breathlessly, and her aunts groaned.

"Not for many, many years, sweetie." Tempest hugged the little girl who'd brought her back home. "First college. Then we'll see."

Cat touched the fabric with one finger. "It is so beautiful."

It was a perfect gown, but then again, it was a perfect day. Rancho Diablo was abloom with Fiona's special touches, and come evening, lots of white twinkly lights would make the grounds a romantic fantasy. Bows and flowers adorned chairs set out for the guests. Looking out the upstairs window, Tempest had spied a lovely wedding cake on a lace-covered table, and so many friends milling around chatting that it made her happy to have such wonderful people in her life.

There had been many blessings in their lives, and she could hardly wait to say yes to Shaman all over again. "I love him," she murmured. "So much."

"I know." Chelsea smiled.

"The Phillips brothers are great guys," Kendall said, nodding.

"Shaman's such a good father." Tempest looked in the mirror one last time, adjusting her veil.

"We're going to take Cat across the hall and put the sparkly barrette in her hair," Chelsea said. "It'll give you a moment of calm."

Tempest smiled warmly, then said, "You're beautiful, Cat."

The teen beamed. "Thanks, Aunt Tempest." She followed Chelsea and Kendall out the door, practically skipping with excitement.

Then Tempest was alone, her first moment by herself since she'd gotten dressed. She looked down at the stunning engagement ring Shaman had given her, a sparkling two-carat oval he said represented the two precious sons she'd given him. Then she closed her eyes, thinking about what a wonderful day today was, and how much it meant to her that Shaman wanted to be her husband, wanted to be with her for the rest of their lives.

She opened her eyes and found him standing behind her, smiling at her. He was the most handsome man she'd ever seen. She turned to tell him how much she loved him—and realized she was alone in the room at Rancho Diablo.

And then Tempest knew the legend was true. There was a difference between make-believe and the magic of love.

And she was truly in love with her cowboy soldier.

SHAMAN THOUGHT HIS HEART was going to beat right out of his chest as first Cat, and then Kendall, and then Chelsea walked to their places. And finally his gorgeous bride walked down the beribboned pathway to the altar.

Tempest looked like a fairy princess, and he could hardly believe she was all his. He hoped the photographer was snapping photos like mad because he wanted their sons to see how beautiful their mother was on her wedding day. She was on Shinny's arm, and her stand-in father looked as proud as he could possibly be.

Millicent and Fitzgerald were smiling from the first row, and Shaman thought his mother might even have tears sparkling in her eyes, which was surprising, because she'd never been sentimental.

They had all changed so much, and he appreciated those changes as only a man whose heart had been touched could.

Tempest walked toward him as Diablo's string quartet played a soft bridal march, and then she was at his side, smiling up at him. "You're so beautiful," he whispered. But he must have said it too loudly, or the words were picked up by the deacon's microphone, because the guests laughed with pleasure at his compliment.

Tempest gazed into his eyes. "I love you, Shaman Phillips."

"I love you, Cupertino. You're the magic in my life."

"I should probably start the ceremony," the deacon teased.

Shaman grinned as widely as he ever had in his entire life, except for when he'd realized that he was a father to two wonderful babies. Tempest had brought him so many good things.

Suddenly, Shaman thought he heard the sound of Rancho Diablo's famous Diablos running through the canyons, a portent of magical things to come, and peace washed over him.

Tempest's eyes widened, and he knew she'd heard them, too. "Magic," she whispered.

Shaman just smiled. He knew all about magic, and Tempest and the boys were the magic he'd finally found after so many years of searching.

Wonderful, beautiful magic. Forever.

* * * * *

REQUEST YOUR FREE BOOKS!
2 FREE NOVELS PLUS 2 FREE GIFTS!

♦ Harlequin

American ★ Romance®

LOVE, HOME & HAPPINESS

*What happens when a Texas nanny learns she is
the biological daughter of a prince? Her rancher boss
steps in to help protect her from the paparazzi, but who
can protect her from her attraction to him?*

Read on for an excerpt of
A HOME FOR NOBODY'S PRINCESS
by USA TODAY bestselling author Leanne Banks.

Available October 2012

"This is out of control." Benjamin sighed. "Well, damn.
I guess I'm gonna have to be your fiancé."

Coco's jaw dropped. "What?"

"It won't be real," he said quickly, as much for himself
as for her. After the debacle of his relationship with Brooke,
the idea of an engagement nearly gave him hives. "It's just
for the sake of appearances until the insanity dies down.
This way it won't look like you're all alone and ready to have
someone take advantage of you. If someone approaches
you, then they'll have to deal with me, too."

She frowned. "I'm stronger than I seem," she said.

"I know you're strong. After what you went through for
your mom and helping Emma to settle down, I know you're
strong. But it's gotta be damn tiring to feel like you've
always got to be on guard."

Coco sighed and her shoulders slumped. "You're right
about that." She met his gaze with a wince. "Are you sure
you don't mind doing this?"

"It's just for a little while," he said. "You mentioned that
a fiancé would fix things a few minutes ago. I had to run it
through my brain. It seems like the right thing to do."

She gave a slow nod and bit her lip. "Hmm. But it would cut into your dating time."

Benjamin laughed. "That's not a big focus at the moment."

"It would be a huge relief for me," she admitted. "If you're sure you don't mind. And we'll break it off the second you feel inconvenienced."

"No problem," he said. "I'll spread the word. Should be all over the county by lunchtime. No one can know the truth. That's the only way this will work."

Coco took a deep breath and closed her eyes as if preparing to take a jump into deep water. "Okay" she said, and opened her eyes. "Let's do it."

Will Coco be able to carry out the charade?

Find out in Leanne Banks's new novel—
A HOME FOR NOBODY'S PRINCESS.

Available October 2012 from Harlequin® Special Edition®

HARLEQUIN *Romance*

At their grandmother's request, three estranged sisters return home for Christmas to the small town of Beckett's Run. Little do they know that this family reunion will reveal long-buried secrets… and new-found love.

Discover the magic of Christmas in a brand-new Harlequin® Romance miniseries.

In October 2012, find yourself
SNOWBOUND IN THE EARL'S CASTLE
by **Fiona Harper**

Be enchanted in November 2012 by a
SLEIGH RIDE WITH THE RANCHER
by **Donna Alward**

And be mesmerized in December 2012 by
MISTLETOE KISSES WITH THE BILLIONAIRE
by **Shirley Jump**

Available wherever books are sold.

www.Harlequin.com

HRI7837